Dragonbound VIII
Black Dragon

Rebecca Shelley

Wonder Realms Books

Cover art © Taily_sindariel | Dreamstime.com
Interior art © Rocich | Dreamstime.com

ISBN-13: 978-0692450673

Published by Wonder Realms Books

To Matt (Pyro) Barron and Mike Rogers.
Thanks for all your help!

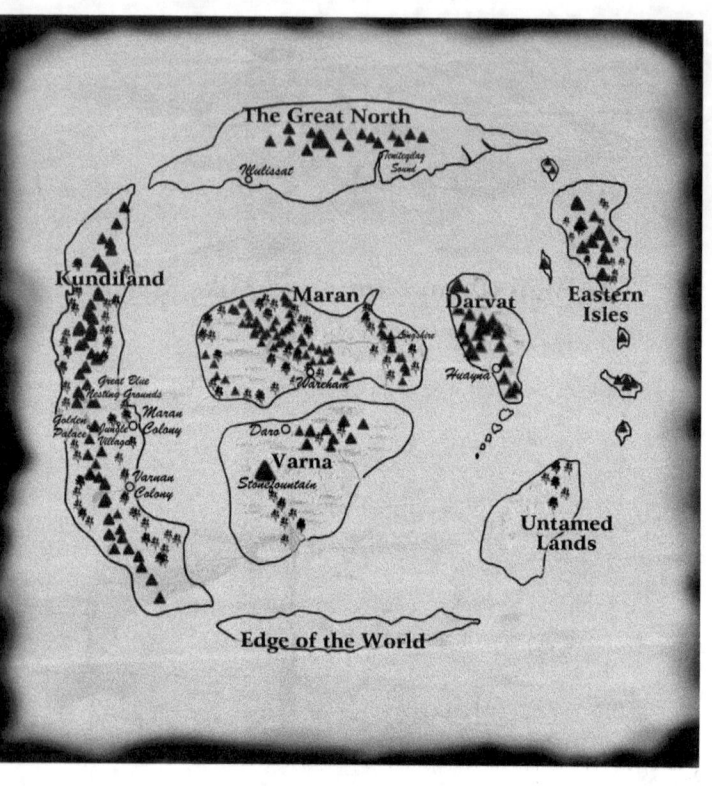

Dragonbound

Prologue

Indumauli snaked up the Black River, leaving the Maran Colony behind. The battle there had been swift and decisive. He'd done his part, tearing the Maran soldiers from the walls on the river side of the colony and disarming them. He'd had to kill two of the humans to protect his own life. A strike with his poisoned fangs had finished them almost instantly. He regretted their deaths only because His Majesty Amar did. He'd left the other six humans alive, and they'd rejoined their commander, General Chandran, in service to the king.

That had been in the morning just before sunrise. Now, the brutal sun had risen into the sky, sending its fire over the jungle, though mist and rain clouds threatened to envelop it. Despising the brightness, Indumauli swam along the bottom of the river in the deepest shadows. With the sun up, the humans were energetic and planning, the jungle vibrant with life. But Indumauli was tired and anxious to return to the cool darkness of his lair.

He passed below the deserted jungle village. Well, not totally deserted. The dragon hunters that had attacked the golden palace were there—dangerous men, the bravest of their kind. These dragon hunters had allowed the Great Blue dragons to carry them into the heart of a battle between the human armies and dragon armies to destroy Rajahansa who had sided with Khalid. These hunters were not to be trifled with. Indumauli was glad His Majesty Amar had not allowed Kumar Raza and Rajan to take control of their minds and use them in the attack against the Maran Colony.

Hidden from them in the depths of the river, Indumauli shuddered. They'd killed Rajahansa, Indumauli's king and long-time friend. Sorrow like burning rays of sunshine swept through him. Rajahansa should not have had to die. Indumauli dug his webbed claws into the mud at the bottom of the river, tearing out great gouges in anguish. *Rajahansa, Rajahansa, why did you turn against your own friends?* he implored the dead Great Gold Dragon King. *What could Khalid have promised you that would twist your heart against those of us who loved you most?*

He received no answer, for ghosts do not speak so easily.

In what place does your spirit rest, Indumauli wondered, *at Stonefountain? If I could find your stone, perhaps I could speak to you one last time, perhaps we could find some reconciliation.*

Only the hollow echo of the river's current responded.

Groaning, Indumauli flicked his body and sped up a tributary to his lair in the heart of the mountain beside the jungle village. He found Aadi waiting, dangling his feet in the underground lake Indumauli called home. Indumauli surfaced and rubbed his scaly head against Aadi's legs.

"Indumauli." Aadi slipped into the water beside him. "You're back. How did the battle go? Did you . . . win?"

We won, Indumauli said. He knew Aadi could not hear his words but the young man would understand the ideas behind them.

Aadi ran a friendly hand down Indumauli's side then drew himself back onto the shore. "Is anyone hurt?"

Vasanti and Bensharie were wounded but have healed. Indumauli crawled up beside Aadi and wrapped his coils around the boy. *I'm tired. Let me sleep now.*

Aadi shuddered. Indumauli could feel Aadi's torment had grown during the hours he'd been away. The boy was in the throes of an agonizing emptiness as if he were deep in the dragon fever, but his skin remained damp and cool.

"I'm going to die if I can't get to the gold dragons," Aadi said. "Being around them is the only chance I have that the fever may start. I was hoping . . ." Aadi didn't finish his thoughts out loud, but Indumauli sensed them in his mind. Aadi had hoped that the Nagas would side with Amar, and one of them would carry Aadi to the gold dragon pride at Stonefountain. So many of the gold dragons were his friends, he was sure they would hide him from Khalid, and he would get the fever and bond with one of them. Aadi's disappointment was as consuming as Indumauli's grief at losing Rajahansa.

Indumauli hissed and uncoiled from Aadi. He'd never before questioned Rajahansa's insistence that the Nagas should only bond with the gold dragons, but with the golds gone and Aadi in such pain, perhaps there was a better solution. He circled Aadi, shivers running along his coils, his mind torn between his loyalty to Rajahansa and his love for Amar and Aadi. *Aadi,* he said, coming to a stand still. *After our minds were linked while you were swimming in the river by the new village, I heard His Majesty Amar tell you that perhaps you weren't meant to bond with a gold dragon. I know that is what you've always hoped for, but things have changed. You and I are fond of each other.*

Aadi jumped to his feet. "What are you saying? I can't understand you clearly. You want me to give up trying to find the gold dragons, is that it? Well, I won't do it. I could never let Parmver down like that, no matter what has happened."

Hissing, Indumauli slumped to the ground. He cared little for Parmver's opinion of Aadi bonding with a Great Black serpent, but Rajahansa would have been furious at Indumauli for even considering it. Feeling guilty, Indumauli rubbed his snout with his webbed claw. His whole world had turned upside down. *I want to go to Stonefountain as well,* he thought.

Aadi started in surprise. "Did you just say you want to go to Stonefountain? Why?"

Indumauli nodded. *To speak with Rajahansa's spirit. I cannot rest without some understanding between us. He felt I betrayed him, siding with Amar against him. But it was not him I fought against; it was Khalid. And it was not me who betrayed him in the end; it was Khalid. Can't you see, Aadi? I can find no peace here.*

Aadi puzzled for a moment over what Indumauli had said then climbed to his feet. "But how will we get to Stonefountain? You can't fly."

I can swim, Indumauli said.

"In the ocean?"

The salt in the water stings my eyes and makes my scales itch. It will not be pleasant, but I can cross the ocean. But you . . . you cannot swim so far. A thought sparked in Indumauli's mind. Silverwave had swum around the world pulling Kumar Raza in a little boat. There were boats in the jungle village, and supplies left behind.

"That's brilliant." Aadi's hands clenched into fists, and he looked around at the solid walls of the rock chamber that housed the lake. "I don't think His Majesty Amar would approve though, and I can't get out of this mountain without his permission. Still, he can't keep me locked down here forever. He'll have to let us out now that it is safe."

The dragon hunters are still in the village. His Majesty will have Karishi keep you down here as long as they are there. Indumauli slid into the water and swam in an agitated circle.

"Wait," Aadi said. "Indumauli, if the mountain is sealed how do you get in and out?"

There is an underground channel that leads from the lake to the Black River.

"Then you could take me out that way," Aadi said.

Indumauli shook his head. *Humans do not breathe under water.*

"I can hold my breath. If you carry me and swim at your top speed we could get free together. I can sneak into the village, get the boat, and we'll be gone. Just don't tell His Majesty where we are and what we're doing until it's too late for him to stop us." Aadi took a deep breath and glanced one more time around the dark chamber. "Please, Indumauli."

Indumauli shook away his desire for sleep. *We should go now. They won't expect me to be doing anything in the daytime besides sleeping in my lair. That will buy us time. Can you shield your mind from the king?*

"Yes. Parmver drilled me relentlessly on that. I miss him."

I miss him too. Come down into the water. Get a good breath of air. You're going to need it.

Aadi slid into the lake beside Indumauli and sucked air into his lungs as Indumauli wrapped his coils around him. When he was ready, Indumauli dove beneath the surface, taking Aadi with him.

Chapter One

LaShawn stiffened as his father's presence slipped from his mind with the ever-so-faint whisper of alarm, *Help me.*

One moment his father had been content—they had found Kanvar's friend, located the Hall, and seeing no sign of Kha-lid's followers, stopped for a quick bite to eat. The next moment his father's mind went dark, the call for help only a faint echo before unconsciousness.

LaShawn jumped to his knees and scrambled out the door of his house. "Damodar," he called. *Damodar, something is wrong.*

Damodar stirred in his cave, stretching as he came awake. *Wrong?*

With my father. He's in trouble. LaShawn clenched his hands and looked down at his right fist in surprise. He unclenched it and clenched it again. It had been a long time since he'd been able to do that firmly. His arm still ached, but it was healed. He had full use of it, thanks to Kanvar.

Kanvar? He snapped his mind out searching for the young prince that had come with his father. LaShawn could not feel him, or Ishayu, his father's dragon. LaShawn's gut wrenched. What would it take to subdue two Nagas and a Great Gold dragon? What danger could they face here?

The humans. Damodar hissed and barreled out of his cave along the well-worn path down the hillside to La-Shawn's house.

If anyone were to see the Great Gold dragon move, they would note how ugly and awkward his stride was. He'd lost his hind legs below the knee when LaShawn had, but that did not stop him now. He stretched his wings as he went. It was flight he had missed for so long. When LaShawn's arm had been crippled by the falling wall that also crushed his legs, Damodar's right wing and fore-leg had been crippled too. But Kanvar had healed that. Damodar flapped his aching wings. They were weak from disuse but with effort they lifted him off the ground. A few moments later, he landed in front of the house where LaShawn waited.

"Yes, the humans," LaShawn said. "Kanvar seemed to trust his friend, but what is friendship between humans and Nagas? Even in Navgarod that's rare. Here . . . I would never trust any human. Uncivilized butchers, all of them."

Damodar growled in agreement. *They will kill your father. It may already be too late.*

"We can't let them do that. Can you fly with me on your back?" LaShawn hobbled over to Damodar and rubbed his golden plates. The sun glimmered off them, warming the smooth gold and half-blinding LaShawn.

If we go to your father's rescue, they'll kill us too. We have no weapons. Your sword hand and my wing are weak, unused for . . . ever it seems.

"You have your joy breath, and unless the humans have singing stones, we should be able to control their minds."

Of course they have singing stones. That's what Kanvar and your Lord Father were sent to get.

"So . . . what? We just sit here and do nothing? Are our lives worth more than my father's, and a prince's, an heir to the throne of Stonefountain?" Terror thrummed through LaShawn. He did not want to face the humans again. He was crippled and useless and could do little good to help his father.

You decide, Damodar said. *If you wish to go, I will try to carry you. I . . . would like to fly with you at least one more time in this life, even if it is our last.*

LaShawn swallowed. *People will see us*, he thought. *They will kill us. Worse, despise us for our crippled bodies.* He would rather die than have anyone from home know his fate.

Still clinging to pride, Damodar said gently.

"What else do we have besides our shattered pride?" LaShawn said.

You have your father's love and your king's acceptance. What else matters? Damodar sank to the ground and lowered his head so LaShawn could climb onto his neck. *But we won't have either if we let Kanvar and your father die at the hands of the humans.*

"You're right, Damodar." LaShawn slipped onto his back, feeling awkward without the lower half of his legs around the dragon's neck to steady him. "I hope I don't fall."

You won't fall. Damodar lifted his head, locking the plate on the back of his skull over LaShawn's lap. He took a deep breath and flapped his wings. LaShawn could feel the strain as he worked hard to lift his body from the ground. Without his lower legs, Damodar could not launch himself into the air to begin the flight.

Next time we should take off from the top of the hill, Damodar muttered as inch-by-inch he worked his way into the air.

LaShawn rubbed Damodar's neck. "Come on. You can do this."

Damodar finally got enough momentum to lift himself above the trees where the updrafts stroked the sides of the hill. He curved his wings into the wind, and with a rush he caught the air and flew.

LaShawn's heart leaped to his throat, and his vision clouded with tears. *We're flying,* he whispered into his friend's mind. *Damodar, you're flying.* All the years of scrabbling on the ground, exerting barely enough effort to survive, not caring to do more than exist, shivered away from him.

LaShawn felt the sun on his face and spread his arms as if they too were wings and could catch the mountain updrafts that flung him and his dragon into the sky.

After a joyous moment, LaShawn caught his breath and lowered his arms. *They went up the River of Death. I saw the place in my father's mind.* LaShawn showed Damodar the path his father had flown earlier that day. Damodar followed it, winging slowly, letting the air currents do most of the work. LaShawn kept his mind searching for his father. Now they were up in the air, he wanted to rush as fast as possible to help, but it was a miracle Damodar was flying at all. LaShawn could not expect his companion to move any faster.

At last, they came over a high ridge and caught sight of the pool of water at the river's head. There were two men down there with white shirts and gold vests. LaShawn sucked in a pained breath upon seeing the uniforms of the Naga guardsmen. He felt their minds as soon as he saw them, and recognized both men. Bendyn and Weston, men he'd grown up with, men he'd trained with for the Elite Naga Guard—those who were considered his father's most loyal and capable men. LaShawn cringed. These men had been his friends once. He did not want them to see him for what he was now, a crippled half man. Though LaShawn was still too high up to hear what they were saying with his ears, he listened to their conversation with his mind.

"The king ordered us to kill them both," Bendyn said. He had his sword out and advanced toward Kanvar and

Lord Theodoric who lay bound and unconscious.

"Wait," Weston said, blocking Bendyn's advance. "We can't kill Theodoric. He's our lord. We've sworn ourselves in service to him."

"He's a traitor to the king." Bendyn pushed Weston out of the way.

"Maybe he is." Weston grabbed Bendyn's sword arm. "But we can't kill him without a fair trial. By the fountain, he's a Naga Lord, not some meaningless human. By the king's own law, he must have a trial."

"The king ordered us to kill them both quickly before they wake. If we do not follow those orders, we are traitors as well." Bendyn freed himself from Weston's hold and stepped up to Lord Theodoric, lifting his sword for a killing strike.

"*No!*" LaShawn yelled, putting all his power behind the command.

Damodar dove at the two men, who looked up at the sound of LaShawn's command in their ears and mind. Damodar did not wait to see if LaShawn's orders had taken affect on the men. He flew straight at them and blew a sparkling burst of joy breath in their faces before settling to the ground beside their dragons. Lord Theodoric's dragon lay unconscious close by, and Kanvar's human friend, Raahi, sat on a blanket, holding a bottle of berry cider. His mind was blank as if some Naga had wiped it away.

LaShawn slid from Damodar's neck and hobbled over to the two men who had once been his friends. Both blinked at him with silly grins on their faces.

"LaShawn," Bendyn said. "It seems you're half the man you used to be."

"Shut up," LaShawn said, pushing past them to reach his father's side. Theodoric's face was pale, his eyes closed, his chest rose and fell in delicate breaths. He'd been bound hand and foot and a gag stuffed in his mouth.

Beside Theodoric, Kanvar moaned and thrashed feebly against the ropes that held him. They'd gagged him too.

"What happened?" LaShawn asked, freeing the gag from Kanvar's mouth and untying him then starting on the gag and ropes that held his father.

Kanvar blinked up at LaShawn, his mind fuzzy. "The cider, drugged." His words came out in a barely audible slur. "Your father drank more than I."

LaShawn snatched the bottle of cider away from the human, meaning to smash it to the ground, but Damodar stopped him with a thought. The joy breath wouldn't keep Bendyn and Weston sedate for long.

"Right," LaShawn said. He took the bottle of cider to the two men who lay giggling close by and ordered them to drink it.

Weston took it from him. "Thank you, LaShawn my friend. But aren't you dead?"

"He's a ghost come to celebrate the rise of the new Stonefountain with us," Bendyn said, swiping the bottle from

Weston and taking a long drink. "Hail Khalid," Bendyn said lifting the bottle before slumping back unconscious.

LaShawn caught the bottle before it fell and gave it back to Weston. "King Amar is alive," LaShawn said, pressing the bottle into his old friend's hand. "My father is not a traitor; he serves the rightful king. Now drink. That's an order."

"As you command." Weston laughed and took a deep swallow.

Shuddering in disgust, LaShawn returned the empty bottle to the lunch basket. By the time he'd finished, Kanvar had struggled to his knees.

"Raahi?" he lifted a hand to Raahi's forehead. "What has Khalid done to you? What has he done?"

LaShawn snatched a silk kerchief from Weston's pocket, wet it in the pond, and went to his father, bathing his face with the cool liquid. "Leave him be, Kanvar," he said as he worked to rouse his father. "His mind is gone. It doesn't matter. He's just a human anyway, and he betrayed you. Human's have no sense of honor."

Kanvar's fist smashed LaShawn in the face before he saw it coming. "Raahi is not *just* a human. He's my best friend. But even if I had never met him before, he would not be *just* a human because every human is *just* as important as a Naga. We are all living beings, and we all have a place in this world. No one is better than anyone else by birth."

LaShawn pressed his hand against his throbbing jaw. "You crippled pile of camdor droppings. My father is the Lord of Navgarod. No human is worth a hundredth part of his life."

"You're calling me a cripple? At least I never used my deformities as an excuse to waste my life away."

"You dare talk to me like that?" LaShawn burned with shame and anger. Shaking in rage he snatched up Bendyn's sword. "I'll run you through."

"Stop." Lord Theodoric spoke in a rough whisper. "Boys, stop. Both of you."

LaShawn dropped the sword. Theodoric had woken, but his face was still pale and it seemed to take all his energy just to breathe.

"Forgive me, My Lord," Kanvar got to his feet. He swayed unsteadily for a moment but managed to stay upright. He looked from LaShawn and Theodoric over to Raahi and then back. "I . . . LaShawn, I'm sorry. I hit you when I should have been thanking you for saving me. You came. I know you didn't want to, and you came to help us anyway. I . . . thank you." He looked back at Raahi. "Raahi's betrayal was Khalid's doing not Raahi's choice. I'm sure of it. From the beginning, Khalid has been two steps ahead of us wherever we go."

Theodoric lifted a shaking hand to grip LaShawn's arm. "We may not have long before Khalid sends reinforcements. Kanvar, you have to get into the Hall now while you still can. I can't do it. Ishayu and I—" He cut off, gasping for breath. "What poison has he given us?"

"It smelled like a sleeping draught," LaShawn said. "Kanvar is recovering, but you drank more, and you're not as young." He did not like to see his father weak.

Theodoric swallowed and closed his eyes. "I'm in no condition to open the way to the Hall. LaShawn, you're going to have to do it."

A lump swelled in LaShawn's throat. "I haven't used my powers in a long time."

"All you have to do is crack the cliff face open, it's not like you're crafting a marble statue." His father gave his arm a squeeze and nudged him away.

LaShawn's jaw tightened and he stood on his knees to face Kanvar. He'd never met a Naga willing to so violently defend a simple human before. Well, his father looked out for the humans he ruled over, but Theodoric would never have punched someone in anger.

"I'm sorry," Kanvar said again. "I'm afraid I have a blue dragon's temper. Not my dragon's fault. I've always been this way. It's probably a good thing I bonded with a blue and not a gold."

LaShawn gazed up at the cliff face. "I have to open that up?"

Kanvar nodded. Ishayu, Theodoric's dragon still lay dazed on the ground.

"And I suppose Damodar is going to have to fly both of us up there?"

Again, Kanvar nodded.

LaShawn groaned and turned to Damodar. "Can you do it?"

Damodar stretched his wings and let out a deep rumble. *Only if you tear it open quickly and there's a good updraft.*

"We'll try it," LaShawn said. "If we fail, we'll wait for Ishayu and my father to recover. But by then Bendyn and Weston may have re-awoken as well."

Follow me, Damodar said, lumbering up the slope away from the pool of water. *We're better off getting some height before we even start this time.*

Chapter Two

Kanvar climbed on Damodar's neck behind LaShawn. Damodar was a large dragon. Had he been at full strength, carrying two men would have been nothing. As it was, even taking off from the side of the hill, Kanvar could feel the dragon's strain as he pumped his wings that were weak from disuse.

You can do it, LaShawn quietly reassured his dragon. *It's not that far.*

Damodar snorted. *It's not the distance.* He winged from the hillside over to the cliff face where he had to assert real effort to stay aloft in front of the cliff. *It's the hovering.*

LaShawn reached for the cliff face, but Damodar could not maneuver him close enough to the rock while still beating his wings. If he'd had his hind legs, he could have landed against the cliff, using his sharp hind claws and foreclaws to dig into the rock and hold him. LaShawn leaned farther out and nearly fell. Kanvar caught him and pulled him back upright on Damodar's neck. Damodar started to shake with the effort of staying in place.

"It's no use," LaShawn said. "I can't reach it. We'll have to land and wait for Ishayu to recover."

"You have to touch the rock to move it?" Kanvar's mind spun. He was so close to gaining entrance to the Hall that he didn't want to give up now.

"Yes, of course. There are some stonemasters in Aesir that could do it from here, but I'm not a stonemaster. I just dabbled a bit with sculpting."

"What if *I* touch it? Could you use my mind to open the rock?"

"Maybe, but you can't reach it either."

"There's a bit of ledge there and a handhold. I think I could do it."

"That's not a ledge. That's a lip of rock maybe two inches wide and a foot long."

"Good enough for me. Damodar, tuck your head down and curl your neck forward."

If I tuck my head down, my neck plate won't hold you in place any longer, Damodar pointed out.

"Exactly. Do it. LaShawn, hold on so you don't fall."

Damodar snorted, tipped his head forward, and curled his neck as close as he could get to the rock and still flap his wings.

Kanvar leaned toward the cliff face and caught hold of a protruding rock with his good hand. Then he swung his legs over to the foothold he'd called a ledge. His heart beat as hard as Damodar's wings as he scrabbled for a moment to get his crippled leg in place so it didn't drag him off the cliff. Sweat beaded on his forehead and slicked the palm of his hand that held onto the rough stone. A glance down showed a dizzying drop to jagged rocks at the edge of the pool below.

Damodar snapped his head back up to hold LaShawn in place and groaned.

Kanvar got himself steady, though it took a lot of muscle and energy to hold himself in place on the cliff. "I'm good here. Land, Damodar, now. LaShawn, my mind's all yours." Kanvar let down his shields and turned his consciousness over to LaShawn, only keeping control of his arms and legs so he could stay clinging to the cliff.

Damodar peeled away and glided to the ground.

LaShawn entered Kanvar's mind tentatively, shielding his memories to keep them private from Kanvar. Kanvar made no attempt to do the same with his own memories. He didn't care if LaShawn saw his life for what it was. He had enough to concentrate on just to keep from falling.

LaShawn enveloped Kanvar's awareness, and the stone Kanvar clung to became a part of his mind in a way that startled him and nearly made him lose his hold. He was used to feeling the presence of animals. He'd never dreamed a mountain could have existence like that. It was ancient and aware. Alive like nothing Kanvar had encountered. It resisted LaShawn's effort to split the rock face open.

This is no normal rock, LaShawn thought in alarm. *It's fighting me. Rock does not fight; it only exists.*

Kanvar's arm shook and his hand began to slip. He pressed his torso and face against the rock to keep his balance. A fear of falling shivered through him. He started breathing too fast and grew lightheaded. *I'm going to fall*, he thought. *I'm going to fall and die. Don't let me fall*, he pleaded with the mountain. *I don't want to die. Let me in. I'm Raahi's friend. Please, I'll keep all your secrets.*

Hold on Kanvar, LaShawn said. *Damodar is coming back for you.*

No. Just open the rock. Use your power. Use mine and Dharanidhar's. Whatever it takes.

LaShawn tried again, bringing their awareness even closer to the mountain's until it felt to Kanvar like the rock itself was a part of him. He no longer breathed or lived and was only a stone statue attached to the cliff face. He was rock. He was the mountain, ancient, terrible, and full of anger at being disturbed. The rock shuddered and moved. A thin rent opened up in front of him, and he lost his hold and fell forward. He tried to crawl inward, but his body was still stone.

LaShawn, I can't breathe, he screamed. *Let me go.*

Kanvar's sense of self snapped back. He gasped, aware once more of living flesh, of blood pumping through his body, of the taste of sweat and tears on his lips. With his good arm, he pulled himself forward through the narrow hole in the mountain.

LaShawn retreated from his mind, leaving him alone except for the anger of the mountain that brooded over him. Inside was pure black for a moment until Kanvar's eyes adjusted to a dim glow on the opposite side of a long chamber. The glow came from a pool of water at the base of a wall of black rock from which water dripped like tears into the pool. A stream ran from the pool, almost the full length of the chamber before it dropped off into the rocks, sliding down the interior of the mountain to flow out at the base of the cliff outside. Six black columns flanked the stream, carved with the images of the spirits of the dead.

Kanvar shuddered and dragged himself to his feet.

Daylight from the small opening illuminated the walls of the chamber. Kanvar gasped. He'd been to Stonefountain and seen the crystals that grew on the walls there. They were beautiful glowing rocks, but they had no value in human reckoning beyond that of singing stones. Not so here—veins of silver and gold streaked the rocks, promising wealth beyond anything Kanvar had imagined. Raw jewels studded the walls: diamonds, emeralds, rubies, amethyst, and others that Kanvar didn't even know the names of.

He stood frozen, unable to move in the face of such wonder. So this was what General Samdrasen had discovered. So much wealth. No wonder Raahi had gone crazy to get back here and protect it. But it wasn't the wealth of the mountain that Raahi cared about. This mountain was so much more. A song like the transcendent beauty of music from the repaired Stonefountain filled the air, carried by the voices of the dead. It was so sublime Kanvar could not fathom interrupting it, but interrupt he must.

Wiping the sweat from his face, Kanvar limped the length of the chamber to the glowing pool. The bottom was strewn with jewels that had been cut from the walls on Samdrasen's orders and returned to the pool by Raahi. It was these jewels that glowed with an inner fire, lighting the chamber with their colors.

Kanvar knelt and reached into the pool. "Forgive me for interrupting," he said. "But I must talk to you."

The song quieted to a low hum, and a face appeared in the water.

Kanvar jerked his hand back, remembering what Khalid had done to Devaj when he put his hands into the water of Stonefountain, how Khalid had raked through Devaj's mind and created a link that had allowed him to corrupt Rajahansa, Haidar, and Liander, and control Devaj so subtly that no one had noticed.

The face of the dead man in the pool vanished back into its stone.

"Can you hear me? Can you talk to me?" he said, clenching his fist and keeping it away from the water.

The song returned full force, thousands of voices singing melodies and harmonies that intertwined in complexity beyond mortal music. Like touching the mountain to move the stone, Kanvar realized that he must touch these spirits to speak with them, but touching them could form an unbreakable bond like Raahi had with this place and Devaj had with Stonefountain.

Kanvar wasn't sure he was willing to do that. He could not know what price he'd pay for it in the end. He'd been counting on Raahi to talk to these spirits for him. The Darvaties believed that if they traveled to the head of the River of the Dead they would lose their soul. Kanvar knelt at the very start of the river. The spirits of the dead frightened him, though their song was beautiful.

"But what price will I pay if I don't get the singing stones?" Kanvar whispered. He plunged his hand back into the water and stroked the stones that glowed there. "We need your help," he implored the spirits. "Your people need your help. The Nagas are coming to enslave them. Only you can keep your people free, and only if you leave the safety of this hall."

The song vanished, and angry whispers of the dead filled the hall. Faces flashed out of the stones in the pool and swirled around Kanvar's hand.

Kanvar flinched but kept his hand in place. "Please. Raahi said that some of you had volunteered to help me fight Khalid. I know it means unspeakable torment for you, but what other choice do we have? I swear by the fountain I will return you to this place once Khalid is defeated."

The face of a Darvati man came to the surface of the pool. He was young and his eyes flashed with the strength of the mountain and the determination of stone. *There are several of us that would suffer the necessary pain in defense of freedom*, the man said. His voice echoed through Kanvar's mind. *But you do not understand what you are asking.*

"Help me understand," Kanvar said.

It is not only the torment of a few at stake. The removal of souls from this hall does not just hurt those taken. Everyone feels the pain: men, women, and children. We are all bound together. If you take some of us, you sentence us all to the same fate.

Kanvar jerked his hand from the water and staggered up. "All of you? Everyone?" He thought of all the stones taken from Stonefountain and all the ones left behind, all the souls who had lived in torment for so long. "Stonefountain. A thousand years, Stonefountain." Kanvar shook his head in disbelief at the immensity of suffering Akshara had caused by clawing the crystals from the walls of the fountain.

"It can't be," Kanvar said, rubbing his hand against his leg as if he could rub off the carnage caused by the fall of Stonefountain. "Akshara is a hero, the Great Blue Liberator. He freed the world from Khalid's tyranny."

The song of the spirits resurged to life, changing to a poignant lament.

"And Khalid is evil. He's pure evil." Kanvar squeezed his eyes closed, but that did nothing to dispel his memory of Khalid summoning the singing stones back to Stonefountain, returning them one-by-one, ending their suffering and the suffering of those who had been left behind at the fountain, healing all.

"I can't . . . I can't do this." Kanvar limped away from the pool, shaking. "I can't do this." *Father I can't do this.* He sent his mind out across the world. Buoyed by the power of the Hall he found his father's mind as easily as if the two stood beside each other.

Kanvar? Amar's startled thought acknowledged Kanvar's presence. *Where are you? Are you all right? You said it was a trap. Can't do what?*

Father. Kanvar was too agitated to get his thoughts into an organized sentence. *Father, I can't.*

Can't what? Kanvar, relax, breathe. Are you hurt?

I'm . . . Raahi drugged me to keep me from getting to the Hall, but LaShawn rescued me. Kanvar pressed his hand against his chest to still his racing heart.

Who is LaShawn? Amar's asked, trying to understand Kanvar's confused thoughts: the swirling images of Khalid, Stonefountain, Akshara, and LaShawn.

I-I can't.

Kanvar, are you hurt or in immediate danger?

No. Kanvar looked around the Hall. He was surrounded by the spirits of the dead. Their voices washed over him. *Maybe I'm dead too,* he thought.

I don't think you're dead, Amar said. *I can feel your heart beating. Just take a deep breath and tell me who LaShawn is.* Amar let his own soothing presence and strength flow into Kanvar, giving him encouragement.

LaShawn, Kanvar said. Yes, he'd much rather think about LaShawn than sort out good and evil, tyranny and freedom. *He's Karishi's father, Lord Theodoric's oldest son.* Kanvar shared his memories of finding LaShawn, learning how he had come to be crippled and living hidden in Darvat, and healing his arm. *I behaved shamefully, but LaShawn came to Lord Theodoric's and my rescue anyway. For the sake of his father, I suppose.*

You said Raahi drugged you? Amar nudged Kanvar's thoughts back to more pressing matters.

Khalid got here ahead of us. He controlled Devaj for so long, and we did not even imagine it. Devaj told me he came here to check on Raahi while I was in Navgarod. But he did more than just check on Raahi, he planted a command in his mind to stop me from getting to the Hall. Kanvar shuddered, thinking about the vacant look on Raahi's face and the emptiness left in his mind after he'd fulfilled Khalid's orders and given Theodoric and Kanvar the sweet-berry cider.

But you're in the Hall now? Amar patiently drew him once more to the present.

Lord Theodoric is still drugged. LaShawn opened the mountain. And the singing stones, can you get them?

Kanvar shivered. Goose-bumps prickled his arms. *No, I can't. I see now why Karishi was so adamant the singing stones be returned to Stonefountain. The price is too high. We can't value the freedom of the living over the souls of the dead. We must leave them in peace. There has been too much suffering already.* Kanvar tensed, ready for argument from his father. Without the singing stones from the Hall, they would have no way of fighting Khalid.

Kanvar. A gentle peace radiated from his father's mind into his own. *If we stoop to evil deeds to defeat evil we have gained nothing. If you feel we must leave the stones in the Hall, then leave them. Karishi and Kumar Raza have discovered something that will aid us in the fight against Khalid. Your grandfather is on his way to Darvat now. Just close up the Hall, find somewhere to hide, and wait for him.*

Kanvar swallowed back his fear. Of course his father would not want the spirits of the dead to suffer. *Thank you, Father.* He eased his mind away from Amar's and found Dharanidhar's. Dhar was bruised and grumpy.

Drugged, drugged. He growled. *I was engaged in glorious battle, and you got yourself drugged.*

Kanvar stifled a laugh. It was good to hear Dharanidhar's voice in his head. *I'm sorry. What battle? Did you win?*

We won, no thanks to you. Kumar Raza, General Chandran, and Rajan had quite a fight of it though, defeating those Nagas.

Wait, did you just say Chandran, and Rajan were fighting alongside each other? Kanvar's heart skipped. Could it be General Chandran had finally accepted the Nagas of Kanvar's family as friends and allies?

Dharanidhar let out a wicked laugh. *No one can argue long with Kumar Raza when he sets his mind to something. Not even*

General Chandran. You should have seen how Raza convinced Chandran to join us. Dharanidhar's memory of Chandran and Kumar Raza sword fighting on the beach flashed through Kanvar's mind.

Kanvar smiled. *Dhar, I wish you were here.*

I think I'll come. There is a lot of work to do in Darvat, and I'm tired of being separated from you. It may take me a while though. I'll have to fly a little bit at a time and bring plenty of medicine with me. Dharanidhar stretched, and Kanvar realized he was perched atop the broken bell tower at the Maran Colony. He could see the rolling blue ocean through Kivi's eyes.

Good, I'll look forward to your arrival. Kanvar let his verbal connection to Dharanidhar's mind slip away and became aware again of the dim chamber where he stood surrounded by the spirits of the dead. He limped back to the pool and slid his hand once again into the water. The spirit he had spoken with before appeared once again.

Well, Naga, do we join you in battle? The man asked.

Kanvar shook his head. "No. I will not be the cause of so much suffering. We must find some other way to fight Khalid."

A smile spread across the spirit's face. *It seems Raahi was right to put his trust in you.*

"Kanvar?" Lord Theodoric's worried voice called in through the opening in the cliff.

Do not let him enter. The spirit vanished from the pool.

Kanvar spun around. "My Lord. Stay where you are. I'm coming."

Kanvar limped across the chamber, and pulled himself through to look out from the tight opening. He found Ishayu latched onto the cliff face with Lord Theodoric on his neck.

"Are you all right, Kanvar? You've been in there longer than seems necessary. LaShawn and I were getting worried," Lord Theodoric said.

Kanvar blinked in the bright sunlight. "I'm alive, I think." Had he lost his soul in the Hall, or found it? "You've recovered it seems," Kanvar said, relieved to see Lord Theodoric astride his dragon.

"We're still a little shaky. Can you get out? We should leave this place. Bendyn and Weston will wake soon. I've altered their minds so they've forgotten they saw us here. It will be better that way. Khalid won't know we've got the singing stones."

Kanvar grimaced, squirmed out of the hole and accepted Theodoric's hand in mounting Ishayu. "Good idea. But Raahi's whole village saw us arrive, remember? And you spoke to Raahi's father. You can't make them all forget, can you? Should you?"

"I can if your father commands me to. It seems like it should be done. If Khalid knows we have the stones, he could take measures to counter them." While Theodoric spoke, he pressed his hand against the cliff and closed the mountain. The mountain, still vaguely present in Kanvar's mind, snapped shut with gusto. Ishayu flew down and landed beside Damodar who still carried LaShawn on his neck. Raahi sat close by, his mind empty. All signs of their picnic lunch were gone. The basket, food, blanket, and ropes that had bound Kanvar and Theodoric were packed up on Damodar's back.

"My father would never command you to interfere with any human's mind," Kanvar said. "On the other hand, he did just order us to hide and wait for Kumar Raza. Hiding does imply not letting people know we're here." Kanvar pressed his face into his hand. "I don't know, My Lord. I can't tell what's right and wrong anymore."

Theodoric rested a hand on Kanvar's shoulder. "You seem shaken."

"I've been in the realm of the dead, speaking with ghosts. Yes, I'm shaken. And you should know, I failed to get the singing stones. The price was too high, and my father decided we must find some other way to fight Khalid."

Theodoric squeezed Kanvar's shoulder and dropped his hand. "I trust your father's judgment. We are to hide, you say?"

"Yes, but we need to take Raahi with us. I've got to find some way to restore his mind. I can't leave him here. Who knows what your men will do to him."

Lord Theodoric glanced at Bendyn and Weston lying unconscious on the ground. "They're good men, Kanvar. They're just confused right now. They've taken oaths of service both to me and the king of Stonefountain. The

problem is we don't agree on who that king is. I wish—"
Theodoric shook his head. "Things have not turned out like
I thought they would when I set out to aid King Amar."

"Are we leaving then, My Lord Father?" LaShawn
interrupted.

"Yes," Theodoric answered. "We will return to your
home. You've hidden there long enough that I doubt
anyone will find us there now. Ishayu, please bring Raahi,
carefully. He is dear to Kanvar. I'll see what I can do for
his mind when we are safe."

"And the villagers and Raahi's father?" Kanvar asked
as Ishayu lifted Raahi in his foreclaw and took to the air.
Damodar followed slowly.

"I'll take care of the villagers' memories of us as well,"
Theodoric said. "But don't worry; it won't hurt them in any
way. I would not wish to upset your father."

Chapter Three

General Chandran stepped into the longboat where six of his men waited to row him up the Black River.

Standing on shore, Amar extended his arm to Chandran. "Good luck."

Chandran clasped it in goodbye and then slid his helmet onto his head.

Amar winced, which made Chandran chuckle. "You'll be gone from the colony by the time I get back down here with the dragon hunters?"

"Yes, General. Thank you for your help. I'm glad we got to work together." Clouds had moved in overhead, and raindrops clung to Amar's dented gold armor.

"As am I," Chandran said. "Give Kanvar my regards. You're sure he's all right?"

"He said he is, but we'll have no singing stones to aid us. Do you think you can raise an army strong enough to make up for not having them?"

Chandran frowned and ran his fingers along the edge of the iron spear he had strapped to his back. "We'll have to. Just be ready to do your part when the time comes."

Amar nodded and stepped away from the riverbank. "I will. We all will."

Chandran shuddered. He did not relish any Naga getting in Rajan's way when the bloodlust came upon him. Chandran's stomach still churned from watching him shred the Nagas they'd fought at the colony. He'd not seen Rajan since then, though Amar said he was close by with his serpent. Amar was a good man, a kind man, but useless in battle. In contrast, Rajan. . . . Chandran shook his head. Rajan would be a valuable asset in their war against Khalid, but Chandran was glad he was headed far away from Kumar Raza's brother.

Chandran sat down in the boat and motioned for his men to begin rowing. Four of the soldiers took to the oars. The other two readied their crossbows and kept watch for dragon attack from shore. They were going up into the jungle where not so long ago an army of thousands of lesser dragons had confronted the human forces. Amar claimed the river passage was clear now, but Chandran's men knew the jungle was never a safe place.

"Remember your orders," Chandran told his men as they made their way upriver. "Do not speak to the dragon hunters about what happened at the Maran Colony. I will give them the information they need to know, and you will keep silent, all of you."

"Yes sir," the men responded.

Chandran would prefer that Qadim and the other dragon hunters never found out that Amar, Kanvar, and Rajan still lived. No doubt it would only take the merest of thoughts by Rajan to erase that information from the minds of Chandran's soldiers. As tempting as that was, Chandran was glad Amar was the type of man who would be scandalized by such a suggestion. No, Chandran would have to trust his men to follow orders.

The rain clouds dropped lower and wisps of fog condensed on the river, giving a ghostly aspect to the carcasses of the slain dragons and dead soldiers along the edge where the combined Maran and Varnan army had pressed upriver. It had been a bloody battle, all the humans against all the dragons, and all of it a diversion so the Great Blue dragons could carry the dragon slayers to the golden palace where the most important fight had taken place. And the dragon hunters had thought they'd won, killing the Nagas at the palace. With the Nagas dead and the lesser dragons' hunger sated on human flesh, the dragon army had dispersed, and the humans celebrated their victory. But they'd all been fooled by Khalid. The real danger lay elsewhere, at Stonefountain.

Chandran gritted his teeth. His army had not even had time to mourn the dead before the Naga Guard had enslaved them and taken them away to serve Khalid at Stonefountain. The remains of the fallen soldiers still lay on the river bank to be picked over by the scavenging black monkeys. The smell of rotting flesh mixed with the scent of the wet jungle plants.

"How many men did we lose, Meric?" Chandran asked the soldier nearest to him, a good young man whom Chandran had served with for several years at the Maran Colony.

"To the dragons or to the Nagas, sir?"

"To the dragons. We will recover the men taken by the Nagas."

"Not if Kanvar didn't get the singing stones," the soldier said. "I still can't believe he's a Naga. Your little crippled servant, a Naga."

"Bound to that terror of a Great Blue dragon, no less," one of the other men added. "He should be our enemy."

"Yes, but we need all the allies we can get," General Chandran said.

The soldiers fell silent.

"How many men, Meric?" Chandran pressed.

"We never got a final count, hundreds for sure, maybe a thousand," Meric said. "The Varnans lost more. Their soldiers aren't as well trained for fighting in the jungle as we are. The dragons were . . . they've never been like that before, like they were ravenous and only human flesh could fill them. I hope never to see the likes of it again."

Chandran grimaced. He'd known there would be heavy casualties, though he didn't like to think of so many men fallen, so many families back in Maran who would never see their beloved sons and fathers again. His army had been decimated by the dragons. The survivors, along with the remaining men of the Varnan army, had been turned against him. By Kumar Raza's count, Khalid now had dozens of Nagas as well. How could Chandran fight them without the singing stones to free his men? There seemed little hope.

Chandran listened to the raindrops patter against his helmet as the fog on the river thickened. He brushed his fingers against the cool wet metal. A slim hope. A fool's chance. A chance he had to take, though the army he'd be building would be untrained citizens, anyone and everyone he could gather in secret and arm for war. He'd need more than double the number of Khalid's forces to make up for his own army's lack of skill in battle.

"General," Meric whispered. "I think there's someone on the water. A boat, there in the mist." He pointed ahead of them and to the side. Something black moved in the fog, sliding beneath the overhanging branches and vines near the river bank and disappearing from view.

General Chandran unslung his crossbow and loaded it. "Who's there?" he called. "Identify yourself."

The water splashed and a black coil rose above the surface close to the boat and then sank back down. Meric swore, jumped to his feet, and aimed his crossbow at the water. "It's the Great Black serpent."

The rest of the men readied their weapons as well.

"Hold," General Chandran ordered. "That serpent is supposed to be on our side."

"It killed two of us at the colony," Meric said.

"On my command, while you were being controlled by the Nagas." Chandran's hand tightened on his crossbow. He had no Nagas with him to communicate with the serpent now.

"All right then," Meric said. "Tell it to leave us alone."

"In-Indu . . ." Chandran fumbled to remember the serpent's name. "Indumauli?"

The serpent's head rose out of the water beside the boat. Its eyes were inky black, and its dragonstone pulsed in the fog.

"We are allies," Chandran said. "You know we are allies, right?"

Indumauli nodded.

"It's daytime. I thought you'd gone to your lair."

Indumauli motioned with a webbed foreclaw at the cloud-darkened sky and fog on the river as if to say he had no fear of the sun at the moment.

"I can't believe you're talking to a Great Black serpent," Meric muttered.

Chandran waved him to silence. "Let us pass. We're on business for King Amar."

Indumauli nodded and sank back into the water.

Chandran let out a relieved breath and ordered his men back to rowing. That serpent could have overturned their boat in an instant and killed them all a moment later.

"I don't like this," Meric said. He remained on his feet, his weapon ready.

Chandran could see the tension and fear on his men's faces. The entire army had forged up this river and barely made it to the village. Now General Chandran had asked them to go alone with him, only six soldiers and the General against a jungle full of dragons that wanted them dead.

"We'll be all right," Chandran reassured his men. "The Naga King rules this land now that the Varnan dragon hunters and I have slain those who tried to usurp his throne. The dragons of Kundiland, lesser and great, will obey King Amar's commands."

"But we can't trust him," Meric said. "A golden king in golden armor. He's a Naga. He can do whatever he likes with us, and we can't stop him. We should go back and kill him now while we have the chance."

Chandran chuckled. "Meric, the fact that your mind is free to think about killing the king proves that King Amar is not controlling you. But you're right about one thing. He could have done whatever he liked with us. He could have enslaved us or killed us. He had plenty of opportunity to do so. The fact that he didn't should mean something to you. We are free. If he had wanted to kill us, he would have done so already, not sent us into the jungle to be eaten by dragons."

Meric sank to the bench but kept his crossbow loaded and ready. Probably a good idea. Amar was unlikely to be keeping track of every lesser dragon between the Maran Colony and jungle village.

After what seemed like forever of rowing, a limp Maran banner came into view on the riverbank ahead. "There's the marker," Chandran said. Raahi had let slip the location of the jungle village to Chandran during a casual conversation back in Darvat. Chandran allowed himself a faint smile. Raahi was trusting and affable, and Chandran was fond of the boy. It had never even entered Raahi's mind that he was divulging secrets that could endanger his friends. "Sorry about that, Raahi," Chandran whispered to himself as his soldiers brought the boat to shore.

Hidden high in the canopy, the jungle village was near invisible in open daylight. Only careful observation by scouts with a spy glass had pinpointed its exact location. Chandran and his men would have missed it now in the fog if the army had not planted the marker on shore.

The men climbed out and pulled the boat up onto the riverbank.

Chandran turned away from the river, and a wet rope slapped him in the face. He pushed it away. It swung back, and he realized it was hanging from a platform high over his head. A matching rope hung down several feet away.

"Looks like someone let a boat down from the village," Meric said. "I never got this far, but reports were that the village was deserted. There were boats on the platform above the river. Primitive huts, abandoned. None of our men remained here after the Nagas took control."

Hair prickled on the back of Chandran's neck. "But someone let down a boat. The Great Blue dragon brought Qadim and the dragon hunters here after the Nagas started for Stonefountain."

"Perhaps it was the dragon hunters then," one of the other soldiers said. "They've taken a boat and left. We saw something on the river, remember? It could have been them."

"No," Meric shook his head. "They couldn't have all gone, not in a village boat. Ten men in a single dugout canoe that could barely hold two or three? If we passed someone on the river, it couldn't have been more than a couple of men Qadim sent to scout."

"There's only one way to find out," Chandran said. "I don't suppose any of our men left a rope ladder hanging here somewhere?"

Meric shook his head. "They left the marker. That's all."

Chandran looped his hand through the rope and tugged, making sure it was secure. It held. "Stay here and keep watch," Chandran told his men. "And remember, when I bring the dragon hunters down with me, you keep your mouths shut about King Amar. We have his aid only as long as we keep that promise. Khalid and the Naga Guard are enemies enough for now. Let's not make Amar an enemy as well."

The men agreed. They had their doubts about working with Nagas like Amar, Rajan, and Tana, but they understood that it was those Nagas who had freed them from Khalid's enslavement.

Taking a deep breath, Chandran started up the rope. As a younger man, climbing a rope had been easy for Chandran, even laden with weapons as he was now: sword, crossbow, harness, bolts, spear, and armor. "By the fountain, I'm an old man," he muttered through gritted teeth as his muscles started to burn a quarter of the way up. Should have sent Meric to fetch Qadim down here. But Qadim would have laughed at that. Though Qadim was even older than Chandran, Chandran was willing to bet Qadim could scale the rope several times before getting short of breath.

Halfway up, Chandran had to pause and catch his breath. Why did they have to put their village so high off the ground?

"You all right, sir?" Meric called up to him.

"I'm fine, Meric." Wipe that smirk of your face, young man, he thought. Wait until you get my age and see how you do. He started climbing again, and after a few more rests, finally reached the top and dragged himself onto the platform.

He lay there for a moment looking up at the leafy branches swathed in mist above him until his arms and legs stopped shaking. Why couldn't Khalid have come back to life while I was in my twenties? he mused. I'm supposed to be retired. Could have used that Great Green dragonstone to buy me a nice little house on the coast of Maran and settled down to a life of ease. But no, I had to use it to be all heroic and go after General Samdrasen. Now look where it's got me. He dragged himself to his feet and headed across the platform, past the remaining boats to a walkway leading into the village. By the fountain, they don't even have handrails. This place is creepy. He did himself the favor of not looking down as he stepped across the narrow walkway and onto the next platform.

He heard a bolt click into place in a crossbow and froze. "Don't shoot. Its General Chandran," he called. Of course, the dragon hunters would have posted a guard. "Bitterwood, is that you?"

"Yes, sir." Bitterwood, the youngest of the dragon hunters stepped out from behind a round hut and lowered his crossbow. "You're alive? That Great Blue monster didn't kill you? But you and he have been enemies forever."

Chandran shrugged. "We both hate Nagas, especially Khalid, more than we hate each other."

Bitterwood shook his head in disbelief. "Where did he take you? How did you get back?"

"I'll explain everything in just a moment. Where's Qadim?"

"Inside the big hut, there." Bitterwood pointed to a central platform where a larger stick hut dwarfed the others around it.

"Thank you." Chandran nodded to Bitterwood and started for the central platform. Bitterwood slipped back to his post. "Don't shoot my men," Chandran said over his shoulder. "They're on the ground below."

"Yes, sir."

Chandran navigated a few more walkways and stepped thankfully onto the main platform. At the sound of his footsteps on the wet wood, the door sprang open. Two more of Qadim's men burst out, weapons ready, shooting their crossbows as soon as they saw a mark. Fortunately for Chandran, they hadn't taken the time to aim well. One of the bolts glanced off the side of his helmet. The other hit him in the left arm.

"By the fountain," Chandran roared at them. "Put your weapons away. I'm a friend, not a Naga."

"A friend controlled by a Naga is not a friend," one of the men said while they both reloaded their crossbows.

"I'm not being controlled by the Nagas." Chandran put his hand to his wounded arm.

"The Nagas took control of the whole army." The men raised their crossbows ready to shoot again.

"Fool, I was with you when that happened, remember? My mind is as free as yours."

Qadim appeared in the doorway. "Chandran is that you?"

"Yes. Call your raptors off."

Qadim motioned for his men to lower their weapons and stand aside. "Where have you been, General?" Qadim's voice was cold, and his hand rested on his sword hilt.

Chandran gritted himself against the fiery pain in his arm and spoke. "The Great Blue dragon took me to meet with Kumar Raza. We planned and executed an attack on the Naga garrison at the Maran Colony with the aid of several Great dragons. We were victorious and have secured the outpost."

"Impossible. Without singing stones even the Great Dragon Hunter couldn't do such a thing. The Nagas would have simply enslaved you like everyone else." Qadim drew his sword.

"Not impossible. We did it with this." Chandran reached into his belt pouch and pulled out the small iron box that once had contained his singing stone.

"You have a stone? How could you?" Qadim lowered his sword.

General Chandran cleared his throat. "No. I don't have a stone. But we've been blind, Qadim, thinking all this time that the singing stones were our greatest asset in the fight against the Nagas. Kumar Raza showed me differently."

"Wait, isn't Kumar Raza dead?" One of the trigger-happy hunters said. "You told us that crippled Naga boy killed him in the Eastern Isles after he hunted a Great Red volcanic dragon."

"Yes, I said that, and I thought it was true." While their weapons were lowered, Chandran walked past the men into the hut, set the iron box on a table inside, and sat down on a chair beside it. Qadim and the other two dragon hunters followed him in. That made all nine of the dragon hunters besides Bitterwood present and seated in chairs or on mats throughout the large hut.

"We found the dragon's body, and I caught the Naga and killed him," Chandran continued his explanation so everyone could hear. "The Naga boy said that he'd left Kumar Raza on the island, but we never found a trace of Raza. I assumed he was dead, but it seems I grossly under-estimated the Great Dragon Hunter. He found a boat that had been plundered and carried there by the Great Red dragon. And just for the adventure of it, he sailed eastward away from my fleet. He discovered a string of islands and a new continent, and then made his way back to Kundiland where he teamed up with the Great Blue dragon when he learned about Khalid's return."

Qadim shook his head. "How did he communicate with the dragon? How could he tame such a monster?"

"Dharanidhar." Chandran grimaced and went through his pouches in search of Great Dragon saliva. "The dragon's name is Dharanidhar, and he can write, remember? Kumar Raza communicated with it in writing the same way we did at the palace."

"Then why did he take you to Kumar Raza and not the rest of us?" Qadim sheathed his sword and fingered the iron box Chandran had placed on the table.

"Because you're dragon hunters . . . dragon hunters. He's a dragon."

Qadim slammed the iron box back onto the table. "Yes, and you're his worst enemy. You fought him for decades. What aren't you telling me, General?"

Chandran swore and tore the crossbow bolt from his arm, not bothering to answer Qadim's question until after he'd slathered the wound with dragon saliva. Treating his wound gave him a moment to think. Qadim wasn't buying Chandran's story. Time to try something else. As the wound started to close, Chandran cleared his throat. "Tana. The Great Blue dragon is allied with Tana, remember? The Naga girl bound to that Great Green dragon that snatched her and escaped from the palace before we could kill her. They are friends, Tana and Dharanidhar. Remember, it was she who arranged for the Great Blue dragons to assist us in fighting the Naga King."

"She's still alive?"

"Of course she's alive. We killed the gold dragons, not her green one. And right in the middle of our negotiation with the Great Blue dragon at the palace, Bitterwood had to go spout off about killing every living Naga, which by default includes Tana, Dharanidhar's friend. Why do you think he went on a crazy rampage like he did? He made up his mind that he would have nothing to do with any of you, so he dumped you here at the village and took me alone to a war council with Tana and Kumar Raza."

Chandran pulled out the cloth he kept for wiping his sword blade, cleaned the blood from his armor, and tossed the cloth onto the table beside the singing stone box. "You are asking stupid questions that are beside the point."

Qadim glared at Chandran. "What's the point?"

"The point is that Kumar Raza and I defeated five Nagas at the Maran Colony."

"With Tana's help. She kept your minds free."

"Tana? You think a child, just barely bonded could overpower five adult Nagas who have been developing their power for a couple of hundred years at least? No, she didn't. She did free my soldier's minds after the Nagas were dead. But no, she could not have fought them. Raza and I used this." Chandran picked up the iron box and twisted it back and forth in front of Qadim's face.

"You used a box?" Qadim said. The other dragon hunters that were gathered in the room snickered.

Chandran shook his head and eased the lid off the box. "We've been blind, Qadim, so very blind. Why do we keep the stones in iron boxes?"

"Tradition," Qadim said. "Akshara, the Great Blue Liberator, made the boxes for all the singing stones he originally harvested from Stonefountain to use in the great uprising."

Chandran chuckled and ran his fingers along the inside of the box. "Tradition. And we never once asked why Akshara fashioned boxes for the stones. It must have taken a long time to make them, doing it in secret, keeping the Nagas who could control his mind and read his thoughts from finding out. It seems like it would have been much easier to just tear the stones free and go on a rampage."

Qadim's brow furrowed and his eyes turned thoughtful. The other dragon hunters whispered to each other. Chandran gave them a few moments to think it over.

Qadim's frown deepened. "I don't know what you're getting at, General."

"No?" Chandran leaned forward. "Because you're a dragon hunter, not a military man. There were a lot of Nagas back then, more than Khalid has now. Even if Akshara's mind was free, the Nagas would have shot him down as he tried to escape the palace with the singing stones to free everyone else. He had to sneak the stones out of the palace. He had to free the enslaved population secretly and arm them. He had to build an army large enough to sweep over the city and kill all the Nagas at once, and he had to do it without the Nagas ever finding out. Keeping secrets from people who can read minds is a difficult thing. It's a wonder he pulled it off. And the stones, the Nagas can hear them screaming from some ways away. We can't, but they do. How could he hide that?"

Chandran held out the box and lifted his chin.

"The boxes?" Qadim said slowly.

"Iron boxes, specifically. Akshara must have discovered that iron blocks the singing stones. Stones incased in iron have no effect on the Nagas. They can't hear them. They can't feel them with their minds. It's like they don't exist." Chandran grinned and set the box on the table as the light started to come into Qadim's eyes. "Kumar Raza just took that knowledge one step further."

"What? How?"

Chandran had all the dragon hunters with him now. Time for the final revelation, the truth Karishi had revealed to Chandran, Raza, and Amar down in his lair. Of course, Chandran had no intention of mentioning Karishi. Kumar Raza would forever after be the one to take credit for it.

"The stones block the Naga power. Iron blocks the stones. Therefore, Iron disrupts Naga power as well." Chandran reached over his shoulder, pulled the iron spear free from the harness, and set it on the table next to the iron box. "We tested it. Poor Tana. Just a little cut. She's such a beautiful young woman. Nagas wounded by iron weapons cannot be healed with Great Dragon saliva. You and I, yes. The Nagas, no. The Gold dragons' ability to heal themselves and their Nagas simply by licking the wound closed during battle is no longer a problem. You hit them with an iron spear or crossbow bolt, and they're done."

Several of the dragon hunters jumped to their feet and came over to the table to inspect the spear. "You tried it? You used it on the Nagas?"

"The Nagas at the Maran Colony are dead. Raza and I killed them. The iron weapons work effectively." Good thing the dragon hunters couldn't read Chandran's mind and add the images of Rajan shredding the man he'd killed as well.

Qadim pushed the other hunters away from the spear and leaned down to get into Chandran's face. "That doesn't explain how you kept the Nagas from taking control of your mind, General. If the Naga girl wasn't strong enough to stop them, how did you do it? For all we know, you're under Naga control right now and feeding us the lie they've planted in your mind. They could be very much alive and planning an attack on this village as we speak."

Ignoring Qadim's animosity, Chandran eased the helmet from his head and shook his hair out. "Like my new helmet? Lovely isn't it? Not blue dragonscale like I used to wear. This one's iron. Tana says, when I put it on, it feels like I've died. I cease to exist in her mind. She can't feel me, can't read my thoughts. She can see me with her eyes, but I've vanished from her mind. What's more, when I wear it, it blocks her ability to control me in any way. As long as I have my head incased in iron, my mind is as safe as a singing stone hidden in an iron box."

Qadim grabbed the helmet and held it tight in shaking hands. His eyes flared with excitement. "We can fight him. We can fight Khalid and the Nagas and defeat them. Chandran, do you know what this means?"

"Yes." Chandran rose to his feet. "It means we have a lot of work to do. Secretly, carefully, building an army one man at a time. Freeing their minds and arming them. But we have to move slowly and work in the shadows. The Nagas must not find out about this until we wash over them and destroy them all at once just like Akshara did."

Chandran returned the spear to the harness on his back, tucked the iron box and cloth into their pouches, and lifted the helmet out of Qadim's hands. "I have a boat in the harbor. I will take you and your men to Varna, and you will begin to build there. I'll go to Maran and do the same. Kumar Raza is already on his way to Darvat. He has an army there that he used to free Huayna. That was a bloody mess General Samdrasen caused and I got stuck cleaning up. In any case, it's time to go. Get your gear and meet me by the river."

Grinning, Qadim and the dragon hunters scrambled into action.

Chapter Four

Amar leaned against Bensharie near the Maran Colony's ocean-side gate. "The skies weep," he said. "I feel I could cry with them." Vasanti and Tana had reported the number of dead along the river as they made their way through the jungle toward the village. So much death, and all of it meaningless. Nothing had been gained on either side.

Bensharie snorted and continued to write in the mud with the iron spear he carried.

> Clouds of darkness envelope the world.
> Hope fades.
> No man can fight the coming night.
> No soul can stay the setting sun.
> We turn puzzled faces heavenward and wonder
> Who will be left alive
> When dawn returns?

"You know the rain's going to wash that all away don't you?" Amar said.

That's the irony of it, Your Majesty. We think the way everything is right now is so permanent, that things can't possibly change for the better. But the world always changes. The sun always sets and rises. The rain always washes away what was and leaves new earth for us to write on.

Amar rubbed Bensharie's slick shoulder plate. "You're trying to make me feel better?"

I'm just pointing out that even though the worst possible thing we could ever imagine has happened, in our own lifetime no less, it's not the end. It's only the beginning of our search for a new day.

Amar grimaced. The fog had settled thick over the jungle, but the wind from the ocean sent it swirling in eddies along the beach, sometimes hiding the gray water beyond, sometimes revealing it. Amar rubbed his eyes and sent his thoughts out to the jungle looking for Tana's. She met his mind readily.

General Chandran and the dragon hunters just left the village.

Good, we'll meet you on the cliff. Amar drew himself upright and rolled his shoulders. "I guess it's time."

Yes. Are you going to go get Rajan, or should I? Bensharie asked.

Amar winced. He could feel Rajan's dark presence brooding down the beach a ways. "I have to deal with him somehow, sooner or later."

You have to deal with yourself, you mean? Bensharie said. *You still blame him for everything that happened with Rajahansa, for all the killing, all the death. It's his fault the human armies came here, forcing Rajahansa to turn to Khalid for help.*

"It's the red dragon's fault." Amar clenched his fists.

You say that, but you don't feel it.

Amar shook his head. He couldn't get the images of death and carnage he'd seen through Tana's mind out of his own. "Bensharie, so many people died."

I'll go get him. Tell Dharanidhar to fly you up to Karishi's lair. Bensharie tucked the spear under his forearm and leaped into the air.

"No wait. I'll do it. I do have to confront him . . . confront myself, as you say, sooner or later. Might as well be sooner. Just give me a minute to talk to him. Then we'll go together, you and I."

Bensharie settled back to the ground and licked Amar's dented armor over his heart as if that could heal the anguish he was feeling.

"Thank you, Bensharie." Amar rubbed Bensharie's dragonstone then strode out onto the beach.

Amar found Rajan with his back up against a boulder, his head in his hands, his gruesome steel dragon claws on the ground beside him. Silverwave lay on the beach, half in and half out of the lapping waves building a sand castle next to Rajan, so innocent and beautiful, like a child at play.

Amar shook his head again, still trying to dispel his anguished thoughts. He forced himself to walk out to where Rajan sat.

"It's time to go," he said.

Rajan pulled his head away from his hands and looked up at Amar with naked despair in his eyes. "Your Majesty. I turn myself over to you for judgment and execution."

"What?" Of the many things Rajan could have said, that one never would have occurred to Amar.

"I didn't get the chance to before, but I can't avoid it any longer. I gave an oath in exchange for my brother's life. Well, not his life, but a life worse than death. His back was broken. I promised Captain Vitra I'd give myself up for execution if his dragon healed Kumar Raza's back. I think it took a while for the dragon saliva to sink in though. I'm lucky it worked." Rajan paused, finally taking a breath.

Amar spread his hands in confusion, not sure he'd followed anything Rajan had just said. "Who's Captain Vitra, and why should you have to pay with your life to heal an injured man?"

Rajan let out a dark laugh. "Captain Vitra?" Rajan's lips curled into a snarl as he said the name. "The man you and Bensharie killed."

Amar winced. Vitra had tried to kill Amar even knowing he was the rightful king. "Why did Captain Vitra think you deserved execution?"

"Because I bonded with a dragon other than a gold dragon, because I bonded without Lord Theodoric's permission. Apparently that is an offense punishable by death in Navgarod. Not to mention I openly disparaged Captain Vitra's honor and willfully interfered with the lawful duty of his city guard." Rajan's face twisted into a grim smile. "And I'd do it again too, every day of my life if necessary to save the humans Vitra looked down upon."

"So, I'm supposed to execute you for the very fact that you exist?" Amar didn't like what Rajan was saying and with every word was feeling a bit better about Vitra's death.

"Yes, Your Majesty. Captain Vitra hauled me in for judgment. I couldn't argue the fact that I was indeed not bonded to a gold dragon, so Lord Theodoric ordered my execution. I'd be dead if Kumar Raza hadn't interfered and pointed out that it should be the king who judged and sentenced me rather than Lord Theodoric. Lord Theodoric was relieved about that, I think. I get the feeling there are some laws Khalid left them that Theodoric doesn't approve of." Rajan got to his feet. "You have my sword, and I've set aside my other weapons. I fulfill my oath to Captain Vitra now and turn myself over to you with a full confession." Rajan's face darkened and the despair came back into his eyes. "I am worthy of death."

"Because the red dragon forced a bond with you when there were no other choices? That's not worthy of any kind of punishment," Amar said.

Rajan growled and kicked one of Silverwave's sand towers so it collapsed. Silverwave flicked sand in his face in retaliation. Her silver dragonstone flashed in silent conversation with Rajan. Rajan kicked sand back at her, and she tackled him, pressing his face in the sand for a moment before flicking him over to land at Amar's feet. Whatever the two had been arguing over, they'd kept their thoughts shielded from Amar.

Amar bent down, clasped Rajan's arm, and pulled him to his feet. "I am the king, and I've already proclaimed it is not against the law for a Naga to bond with any Great dragon he or she chooses. Kanvar, Karishi, Tana—you aren't the only Naga to bond with something other than a gold dragon. I wouldn't think of killing any of them, so obviously I'm not going to execute you." The conversation was making Amar feel ill.

"Your Majesty, I'm serious," Rajan said.

Silverwave hissed and knocked the rest of the castle over as she launched herself into the ocean.

Amar sat down on the boulder and stared at Rajan. He was soaked. Water ran down his reddish-blond hair in rivulets, plastering it to his head. Sand clung to his rumpled clothes. His mind was shielded from Amar's, but his eyes were awash in anguish.

"All right," Amar said. "Tell me what it is you've done that you think is worthy of death."

Rajan clasped his hands in front of him and spoke in a choked voice. "Kumar Raza and Silverwave want to believe that everything I did while bound to the Great Red dragon was not of my own free will. That my mind was overcome by the dragon's from the beginning. I've tried to deny it myself for a time, but I know it's not true. I chose to bond with the red dragon. I called it to me after my uncle and father tried to kill me. I felt the dragon's fire and power, and I wanted it. I killed people, Amar. Murdered a lot of people. Shredded them with my claws and feasted on their flesh, and I enjoyed it. Part of me wanted to kill the humans, all of them. I was so angry. My own family had sought my death, because I was a Naga. The humans murder all the Nagas. They show no mercy, no hesitation. They've led a purge and hungered for our extinction for a thousand years. And I decided to fight back. I went to Maran to do that. I can't say if it was the dragon's plan or my own, but I went willingly. I wanted the humans to suffer. I wanted to subjugate and destroy them. I relished the work I did taking over the Maran Senate."

Rajan licked his lips and looked over the water. Silverwave was out there somewhere, but she did not rise to the surface. "I saw into your mind when you refused to perform the wedding ceremony for Dove and me, Your Majesty. I know you blame me for causing the war that destroyed your kingdom and killed your dragon. I know, and so do you, that the deaths of thousands of dragons and humans are laid at my charge. You've watched me fight. You've seen what I am. I cannot hide it from you or myself any longer, and I turn myself over to you for execution. There is no man more deserving of it than I am."

Amar's heart turned to ice, and a raw shiver ran down his spine. He was the king. As king all he'd ever had to do before was settle minor disputes between dragons and treat some sick and injured. Judging a fellow man, sentencing him to death? Amar had no desire for any such thing. But the world had changed. He could no longer spend pleasant days idling his time at the palace with books and music. Rajan was in earnest, and Amar struggling with his own anger and pain. Surely, Rajan deserved execution. Was this justice? The law demanded the life of a murderer. How many innocent people had Rajan killed? Amar could not even begin to guess.

He got to his feet and wondered if Rajan could see him shaking. Justice and death. So many people had died already. He walked out to where the water frothed up on the sand and then rolled back out to sea. Rajahansa was dead. The wind whipped salty water in Amar's eyes. Rajahansa, faced with abandoning his home or dying at the hands of a human army. He'd turned to the only power he'd thought could save him. Khalid had promised him salvation, assured him of victory, and used him as a pawn, leaving him to die brutally at the hands of his enemies.

Amar rubbed his arms, feeling again the pain of the merciless blows. The dragon hunters had meant for him to suffer as he died. But Rajan was right about that. The dragon hunters had started the killing, seeking the destruction of the Naga race. They'd murdered Amar's parents, and his parents were innocent of any wrongdoing. As innocent as a fifteen year old boy dragged out into the jungle to be murdered by his own father.

"So much killing. When will it end?" Amar whispered.

Silverwave climbed out of the rolling water and slid a coil around his legs. She raised her head and torso up off the ground, put a webbed claw against Amar's chest, and stared him in the eyes. She had a scar on her own chest, so much like the one Amar and Bensharie had on theirs, the final death strike that had killed the Great Red dragon. A similar one had finished Rajahansa. Rajan had a scar to match Silverwave's.

Silverwave said nothing. She only looked at Amar. He ran his hand down the slick scales on her chest, feeling the scar with his fingers as he passed over it.

"All right, Silverwave," Amar said. "Let me go."

Silverwave melted away from him back into the water, and Amar returned to Rajan who waited beside the boulder, head bowed. "I have heard all the evidence against you and for you," Amar said. "And I'm ready to give my verdict."

Rajan lifted his gaze to look Amar in the eyes, knowing he was worthy of death.

"Yes, you *are* worthy of death. You are a murderer, a usurper, a criminal responsible for uncountable slaughter." Amar's voice broke. "I would sentence you to death as you deserve if that did not mean also taking the life of an innocent dragon. Silverwave has done nothing but love you. I will not sentence her to death for that."

Rajan recoiled. "I-I didn't mean for her to die."

"Silence. I have given my verdict, but not my final sentence. Since I cannot sentence you to death as you deserve, I sentence you to life."

Rajan's eyes widened in confusion.

"I sentence you to life in my service and charge you with the solemn responsibility to help me defeat Khalid and free the humans you once wished to enslave." Amar gripped Rajan's arm.

Rajan flinched at his touch.

Amar held tight. "Your life is mine from this day forth."

"As you command, Your Majesty," Rajan said in a raw whisper.

The ice that had incased Amar's heart warmed and melted away. He pulled Rajan into a tight embrace. "I forgive you, Rajan. I . . . forgive you."

All the pain and anguish of Rajahansa's betrayal blew away from Amar like mist in the wind. There would always be sadness in his heart, and regret, but the jagged pain he'd carried with him since Rajahansa's death faded. He released Rajan and walked back toward the colony. "Come on. We need to be gone from this place before the dragon hunters arrive. Dharanidhar will fly you up to the cliff above the jungle village."

Amar found Bensharie waiting by the gates where he'd left him. The rain had washed all traces of his poem from the muddy ground. Bensharie licked Amar's face as Amar climbed on his back. Neither of them said anything as Bensharie took to the air. What they shared was beyond words.

A while later, Bensharie landed on the cliff ledge above the jungle village. The crack in the rock leading to Karishi's lair was already open. Karishi and Tana stood together in front of it talking in urgent whispers to each other. They broke off and fell silent as Amar slid from Bensharie's back and walked over to them.

"What's wrong?" Amar asked.

"Aadi's missing," Tana said.

"Missing?" Amar felt the alarm radiating from both Karishi and Tana. He snapped his mind out looking for Aadi and felt nothing.

Karishi blanched. He'd been tasked with protecting the women and children. "Your Majesty, he was down by the underground lake. He couldn't have left the mountain. Everything was sealed up."

"He could have gotten lost in your maze or trapped while exploring some underground cavern. If he's fallen unconscious, we won't feel him." Amar ducked into the opening, anxious to go in search of Aadi.

Karishi grabbed his arm. "I already looked. Tazeran and I have searched everywhere in this mountain, and believe me, we know the mountain. He's not here. Even if he were unconscious or dead we would have found his body unless—"

Tana sniffed and wiped her eyes.

"Unless?" Amar prodded.

"Denali said he last saw him down by the lake. If he fell in, he might have drowned. There is a strong under-current in places. It could have pulled him below the rocks and trapped him where we'll never find his body."

Dharanidhar glided down to land next to Bensharie.

"What's going on?" Rajan asked as he dismounted.

Amar lifted a hand for silence. "I don't know. Give me a second." He sent his mind out again, searching for Aadi. He knew Aadi better than anyone else present. Amar and Parmver had raised Aadi from the time he was very young. He couldn't be dead . . . drowned. Not that. Aadi was a strong swimmer. Amar still felt nothing in the mountain.

"What's wrong?" Rajan whispered to Karishi.

"Aadi's drowned," Karishi answered.

"No," Amar snapped. "He can't be. He can't." *Indumauli?* He reached his mind out to the Great Black serpent that lived in the river and made its hidden lair by the village. Indumauli could search everywhere for Aadi that Karishi and Amar could not. *Indumauli?* The serpent was as strangely absent as Aadi.

Indumauli? Amar broadened his search for the serpent. Aadi might have drowned, but not Indumauli, and Amar knew of no predators that would be a match for the Great Black serpent. Chandran's soldiers perhaps, but Indumauli was too slippery and canny to let them harm him. He'd swum in these waters undiscovered even during the height of the war between the Maran army and Great Blue dragons. *Indumauli?* He knew Indumauli's mind well. They'd worked together for hundreds of years. He felt Indumauli finally, far to the east. Indumauli's mind was shielded from him, but he sensed the serpent's presence, a slippery black force beneath the surface of the water. His skin itched and his eyes burned.

Indumauli, he shouted, using his powers to break through Indumauli's shields. *Where are you? I need you. Aadi's in trouble.*

Aadi, in trouble? Indumauli's bemused response answered.

We can't find him. Karishi thinks he's drowned. I need you back here now to search for . . . his body. Amar didn't want to say it like that. He could not imagine losing the boy after already losing Parmver, Haidar, Liander, Rajahansa, and Devaj.

Your Majesty. A flow of reassurance came from the serpent. *Aadi has not drowned. He's with me.*

You?

He's dying, Amar, and you cannot save him. He needs the gold dragons. I'm taking him to Stonefountain. We know it's dangerous, but there's no other way. It's the only chance he has. Indumauli opened his mind so Amar could see Aadi huddled in the village boat that Indumauli was pulling at top speed across the surface of the ocean.

Aadi? Amar transferred his focus to Aadi's mind. Aadi was capable of far stronger shields then Indumauli, and Amar would not use his power to break into the boy's mind. *Aadi, please. Talk to me.*

Indumauli said something to Aadi, and Aadi jerked up startled, his eyes wide. His mind snapped into contact with Amar's. *I'm not dead. I'm sorry. I never imagined you'd think I drowned. I just didn't want you to try and stop me. I have to go to Stonefountain. Your Majesty, please.*

Connected with Aadi's mind, Amar could feel the sweeping loneliness that nearly overwhelmed the boy. It was as if he were in the deepest throws of the dragon fever. His need to bond was desperate. *You have the fever?*

No. I don't. Despair deepened in Aadi. *How can my soul need to bond so badly and my body not be ready?* He was shaken with desperation and fear.

I don't know, but I fear what Khalid will do to you if you go to him. He's dangerous, and he has no regard for life of any kind, Naga, dragon, or human. Fear for Aadi streamed through Amar.

I'm going to try to get to the gold dragons without being discovered. Indumauli is going to help me.

Amar took a deep breath and spoke again to Indumauli. *I'm putting Aadi's life in your hands. You must keep him safe, whatever it takes.*

I understand, Your Majesty. Indumauli pushed his body to greater speed, driving hard for the Varnan coast and the river that would lead to Stonefountain. Amar pulled his mind away. He was crazy to let Aadi go with only the black serpent to Stonefountain. But who else could Amar send besides Indumauli? Kumar Raza, Rajan, Karishi—everyone knew too much. If Khalid got hold of their minds, the war for freedom would be over before it ever started.

Amar shuddered. Looking around him, he realized that Tana was crying quietly in Karishi's arms. Rajan's face was dark, and blue fire crackled between Dharanidhar's jaws.

"Aadi's not dead." Amar interrupted their grieving. "He's gone with Indumauli in search of a gold dragon to bond with. It's time for him, and what he needs for survival can't be found here. We have to trust him to Indumauli's care."

"The serpent?" Karishi's eyes flashed. "That slippery black serpent snaked Aadi out of my mountain? I knew he made his lair at the lake but—"

"Aadi and Indumauli have been friends for a long time." Amar allowed himself a thin smile. "Besides, if Indumauli's lair is at the lake, then the mountain was his long before you came here."

Tana wiped the tears from her red eyes and backed away from Karishi.

"Go down below, my dear," Amar told her, "and bring the others up. We can stay in the village now the dragon hunters have gone. Tell the others Aadi is all right. I could swat that boy for making everyone worry."

"Yes, Your Majesty," Tana rushed into the opening.

"Karishi, I'm sorry Aadi made your life difficult," Amar said.

Karishi shook his head in exasperation. "I'm just glad he's alive, and I'm not responsible for his death. Tana says your battle at the Maran Colony was a success."

"Yes, thanks to you. I'll need you to show me how to make those helmets before you go. We'll need enough for the people at the new village and our family here at the old." Amar looked out across the jungle. He didn't know if Khalid would send men to retake Kundiland right away or not. If more Nagas and soldiers came, it would be up to Amar, Rajan, and Tana to defend the humans here.

"Before I go where?" Karishi said. "I thought we agreed I got to stay in my mountain."

"Dharanidhar is headed for Darvat. I think you may want to go with him. You have a home there and . . ."

"And?"

Amar grinned. "Kanvar has found your father. He's Lord Theodoric's oldest son, heir to the throne of Aesir. You, my friend, are a Naga Lord."

Karishi blinked, and then his brow furrowed in anger. "I have no parents. I was abandoned. Left to die. Theodoric's son indeed. What kind of a man would discard his own son?"

"A Naga man, crippled, unable to run or fly, pursued by hunters, his young wife torn from him before he even knew she would have a child. A man who has spent every day of his life since then barely able to stay alive. You can choose to hate him if you want, Karishi, but he needs you. You can give him what no one else can."

"What?" Karishi's face softened, but his eyes remained guarded.

"His life back."

Denali dashed out of the hole in the mountain followed by Frost and Miki. "Where's my father?"

"I've sent him to Darvat," Amar answered.

"You sent him away without me? That's not fair. I can fight. I can help him, whatever he's up to." Frost flashed her stone indignantly. Amar barely managed to turn away in time to keep from being blinded.

I can take Denali with me, Dharanidhar rumbled. *And Frost and Miki. It's too hot for them here, and that stupid dog is likely to fall off one of the village platforms and die. This is no place for any of them. Kanvar and Raza can keep Denali out of trouble, and it will be good for Kanvar to have a friend. Raahi is . . . injured and may not recover. Kanvar is not taking it well.*

"Yes," Denali shouted. "Whatever he said, I agree."

Amar chuckled. "How can you be sure he didn't say I should keep you locked in the mountain forever?"

Denali frowned. "It didn't feel like he said that."

"No. You're right. He wants you to go to Darvat. Kanvar needs you." Amar looked up at the monster dragon. "Will you be able to carry so many people?"

Karishi and Tazeran can ride on my back. The others I can carry in a boat like I carried them down from the North. In fact, I think it's best I go back that way, to avoid Khalid's Nagas, and to keep land beneath me as much as possible. I will need to stop and rest often. I will have to carry a good deal of medicine with me in the boat as well. The villagers showed me how to make it, but I doubt the plants necessary can be found in Darvat. It's a nuisance I wish I didn't have to deal with, but— Dharanidhar spread his wings, rolled his shoulders, then tucked the wings back against his sides. *I'm not as young as Bensharie here.*

"Yes." Denali pumped his fist in excitement. "Did you hear that, Frost? We're going to go help fight Khalid."

Mani and Eska came out of the mountain, followed by Vasanti with her wyrmlings clinging to her back.

"You're alive, thank the fountain," Mani said. She ran her fingers over the dents in Amar's armor. "I thought you weren't going to have to do any fighting. My father said he would take care of everything."

Amar took Mani's hand and kissed it. "Things did not go as planned, but I survived and we succeeded. That's what matters."

Chapter Five

Aadi drank a sip of stale water. His face burned from the relentless sun reflecting off the ocean. The boat bobbed in place, stalled while Indumauli slept. The Great Black serpent had dived down far from the sun, leaving Aadi to face its wrath alone. Aadi shaded his eyes and looked out across the endless expanse of heaving waves. We should have reached land by now, he thought. We've been out here for days.

With each passing hour Indumauli had grown weaker and swum slower. The salt in the water was killing him. Indumauli denied it, but Aadi knew it was true. Worse, though Indumauli had insisted he was swimming in a straight line, Aadi had sensed from the serpent's mind that Indumauli was confused. This was no river with one single current. This was endless water everywhere with multiple currents pushing him this way, luring him that way. He was lost; Aadi was sure of it.

Aadi shuddered. The emptiness inside him had grown into a constant torture. He rubbed his heart and tried to keep breathing. He was alone. Far from the jungle where the abundant living beings had played continually across his mind. The expanse above the water was a vast nothingness. Below the waves, he sensed fish once in a while. There had been more by the coast of Kundiland, but he and Indumauli had left the shoals of teaming fish behind with the sheltering fog.

"Empty, empty, empty!" Aadi shouted. "Go away, sun, and let me die in cool shadows." By the fountain, he wished night would return, so Indumauli would wake and maybe somehow get them to land.

A ripple of human minds jarred Aadi's rant. He turned his attention toward the humans and saw a ship coming, a Maran warship. Its blue and gold flag snapped in the wind. Aadi's heart leaped. He grabbed the oar and started paddling toward the ship. The wind in the sails drove the ship in his direction. As it drew closer Aadi jumped to his feet, waved the paddle in the air, and shouted. He couldn't be sure if the humans in the ships would be friend or foe, but he couldn't stand to sit unsheltered beneath the beating sun anymore. If he was lucky, the humans would be working for Khalid's Nagas and be headed for Stonefountain.

Indumauli, Aadi cried with his mind. *Wake up. Indumauli! We're saved . . . maybe.*

Indumauli woke, but his thoughts were sluggish. *What?*

The warship pushed up a crest of water in front of its bow as it rushed toward Aadi. A shout sounded from its deck. They saw him. Aadi lowered the paddle and took a deep breath as the ship came up beside him. A few moments later, a man in blue dragon-skin armor slid down a rope into Aadi's boat.

"Aadi," General Chandran said, "by the fountain, what are you doing out here?"

Aadi blinked at the old soldier. "I could ask you the same thing. I thought you were in Kundiland with King Amar."

"Sh." General Chandran motioned for Aadi to keep his voice down. "His Majesty has sent me on an important mission," he whispered. "But there are dragon hunters on board with my men that do not know His Majesty is still alive. Or Kanvar. In fact, when you come aboard, it would be best if you pretended not to know anything about the Nagas at all."

"Dragon hunters?" Aadi shuddered. "I guess that means you're not going to Stonefountain."

General Chandran frowned. "No. Is that where you're headed? Why? How did you get out here?"

"His Majesty, King Amar, said I could go. All the Great Gold dragons are there, and I will die if I can't find one to bond with."

Chandran clamped a hand down on Aadi's shoulder. "I don't think Amar would send a child out into the middle of the ocean alone in a small boat like this."

"I'm not alone. Indumauli is with me, sort of. He won't surface in the sunlight, but we do fine at night."

General Chandran looked out across the bright water. "Nope, I can imagine you don't get very far this time of day, but you're going the wrong direction if you're headed to Stonefountain."

Aadi gritted his teeth.

"Do you have a map and compass? Do you know how to navigate across the water? A silver serpent like Rajan's might find its way naturally in the ocean, but I doubt Indumauli can."

Aadi ducked his head and stared down at the paddle. Salt water dripped from the wet wood onto his toes. "I think we're lost."

General Chandran grimaced.

"Hey." A young dragon hunter dropped down into the boat beside Chandran, nearly tipping it over. "Qadim wants to know what you're waiting for. Haul the boy up already so we can find out who he is and what he's doing lost in this ridiculous excuse for a boat in the middle of the ocean. Look at his skin; it's as gray as tree bark. Have you ever seen anyone with dark skin like that? And his boat, it's like the ones at the jungle village. Hey, are you a jungle villager?" He moved to grab Aadi, almost knocking the boat over again, but General Chandran stopped the dragon hunter and steadied the boat by adjusting his own weight to the side.

"Bitterwood. Get back on deck and let me handle this," Chandran said.

Bitterwood scowled. "There is no way this little boat could get this far out with just a boy and a paddle."

Two more dragon hunters dropped down into the boat. One of them pulled Aadi up and held him while the other wrapped a rope around him. The line went tight, and Aadi jerked into the air.

The water beneath the dugout frothed, and a black coil lashed just below the surface.

General Chandran grabbed Aadi as he swung past. "Boy," Chandran pulled him close to whisper in his ear. "Tell the serpent to stay down. He'll be killed if he surfaces, and so will you."

Aadi nodded and relayed his command to Indumauli. *Go down deep. We don't both need to die here, and the dragon hunters won't kill me if they don't find out I'm a Naga.*

Indumauli hissed and sank back into the depths.

General Chandran released Aadi, and he swung high in the air onto the deck of the ship. The dragon hunters and General Chandran followed him up.

"Well, boy, what is your name?" An old gray-haired dragon hunter strode over to Aadi. His eyes were piercing and his brow furrowed in contempt. "How did you get this far out into the ocean in that boat? Rowing like you were, it would take you months to reach land, if you didn't go in circles and never reach it at all."

"His name is Tomlin." General Chandran said, stepping in between Aadi and the dragon hunter. "He's a jungle villager, captured by my army and then taken by the Nagas, but he escaped during the crossing to Stonefountain. He needs shade and rest. I'll see him to my cabin."

Qadim glared at Aadi, but no one stopped General Chandran from leading him below deck into a cramped cabin with a bunk built into the wall, a desk and chair against the other wall, and not much else. Inside was cool and smelled of wood seasoned by the salty ocean.

"Have a seat." General Chandran closed the door behind them and watched Aadi sink down on the bed.

"Are you going to kill me?" Aadi asked. "You know I'm a Naga." He was grateful to be out of the sun for a while, but unsure if General Chandran was really on King Amar's side.

General Chandran crossed his arms over his chest and leaned against the door. "I do not believe Amar would send you to Stonefountain." He spoke softly so no one outside the cabin would hear. "You ran away, didn't you? My men and I saw Indumauli on the Black River, and a boat like yours for a moment in the fog."

Aadi clenched his hands. "Yes, I left without asking, but only because the rest of you were too busy to care about me. But His Majesty knows where I am now and where I'm going and has agreed it's for the best. There is no other way. The gold dragons have gone to Stonefountain. I can't stay in Kundiland or I'll die."

Chandran took two strides across the room and laid his hand on Aadi's forehead. "No fever yet. Besides, you don't have to bond with a gold dragon. No one else seems to need a gold: Kanvar, Karishi, Tana, Rajan, even Denali looks like he's going to bond with a dragon other than gold. It's not worth going to Stonefountain to look for one . . . unless you plan to betray the rest of us."

A dark anger blossomed in Aadi's heart and spread through him. He rose and lifted his head to stare into General Chandran's eyes. "Tana led you to murder Raja-hansa. Rajahansa murdered Parmver. Kanvar betrayed his own family and put all the Nagas in danger to help you humans." Aadi's lips twisted into a sneer, and his eyes stung. "What is betrayal? Who has betrayed whom up to this point? Everyone has turned against everyone. Who do you consider *us*? You are not a Naga. We are not human. The moment we defeat Khalid, you will kill the very men and women you have pretended to side with. Is that betrayal? Yes, betrayal of the Nagas who follow Amar. And if you don't kill Amar and his followers, you will be betraying your own people. That's the problem, General. There is no right and wrong anymore. There is only killing and suffering and pain. I see no difference between you humans and Khalid. You both want the world for yourself and don't care who you hurt to get it. King Amar doesn't want to hurt anyone, and because he is weak, everyone suffers. I don't care what you do with me. Let me go to Stonefountain, kill me, or make me your slave. It doesn't matter. There is no good left in this world anyway."

Aadi clenched his teeth and stopped talking. He'd been holding his anger in for so long it felt good to let it out.

"I think I'll leave taking slaves to Khalid. You will be a guest aboard this ship. I'm headed to Maran and will take you with me. Tell Indumauli to follow us. We'll reach the channel between Maran and Varna soon. There's a freshwater river at Wareham. Indumauli should be more at home there than in the ocean. I plan to take the boat upriver and hide. You can help me do the work King Amar has sent me to do.

Aadi clenched his fists. "I will die. I need a gold dragon."

"Why don't you just bond with Indumauli? It's clear you like each other."

Heat flushed Aadi's face. He'd already had this argument with Amar and Indumauli. Why did everyone want him to be something less than he'd always dreamed of? "I am a Naga. Nagas bond with Great Gold dragons and only Great Gold dragons. I do not care if every other Naga in this world wants to pervert the right way, I will not abandon it."

Chandran scowled. "Even if that means you join Khalid and betray Tana, King Amar, and the rest of your friends?"

"I have no intention of joining Khalid. I'm just going to find my dragon friends, bond with one of them, and hopefully free all of them from Khalid's power."

"You think you can fight Khalid by yourself?"

"I'll do whatever I must to bond with a gold dragon." Aadi jerked open the door and stalked out of the room, heading deeper into the ship. He found a hatch to a lower hold, popped it open, and climbed down into the darkness.

Chandran frowned down after him, but did not follow. "If you side with Khalid, I will hunt you down and cut your heart out whether you are Kanvar's friend or not."

Aadi slid through the crates and barrels of supplies to the far side of the hold, sat down with his back against the wall, and pulled his knees up to his chest. He could feel Indumauli lurking beneath the ship, letting it shield him from the sun and guide him through the ocean.

Don't worry about Chandran. Indumauli's thoughts formed impressions in Aadi's mind. *When we come in sight of land, you can sneak off the ship into the water, and I'll swim you to the Varnan shore. We can work our way from there to Stonefountain unhindered.*

Chandran thinks I'm a traitor, that I'll betray my friends.

Indumauli hissed. *You'll do what you have to in order to survive. General Chandran is no friend to the Nagas, though he pretends to be. He'll see you all killed in the end. Don't waste your energy worrying what he thinks of you.*

Aadi bit his lip. *What if King Amar is wrong and King Khalid is right? Kanvar and Tana helped murder Rajahansa. Doesn't that make them worse than Khalid?*

Indumauli's mind swirled in confusion along with Aadi's. *I don't know. I don't think so. Rajahansa murdered Parmver, killed a helpless old man in cold blood. How could he do that? I don't understand. Rajahansa was never like that before he started talking to Khalid. I think Khalid is evil. You must avoid him at all costs when we reach Stonefountain.*

I may not be able to.

I know. Just don't let him turn you to evil like he did Rajahansa, all right?

Aadi swallowed the lump in his throat. *Let's just figure out how to get to Stonefountain first and worry about how to deal with King Khalid later.*

Indumauli hissed in agreement.

Chapter Six

Kumar Raza's muscles ached from being tense for so long. He rode behind Walinash, sword out, pressed against the Naga's throat. King Amar had ordered Walinash and his dragon to carry Kumar Raza to Darvat to save Kanvar. But as soon as they'd gotten out over the ocean, Walinash's dragon had turned toward Stonefountain.

Kumar Raza had been quick to pull his sword and set it across Walinash's throat. "I told you to head northeast across Maran, not southeast toward Stonefountain. Tell your dragon to fly in the right direction, or I'll kill you both." Kumar was once again thankful for the iron helmet Karishi had fashioned for him. Otherwise Kumar would have no power over the Naga he flew with. It seemed Walinash's vow to follow Amar instead of Khalid only lasted as long as necessary to save his life from Rajan's steel claws.

"We're too far out in the ocean," Walinash said. "If you kill Brisbian and me, you'll drown."

"Then I'll drown content that I have rid this world of one more treacherous Naga. You have no honor." Kumar Raza pressed his blade tighter against Walinash's throat, drawing a thin line of blood.

Walinash shuddered. "All right. We'll take the Maran rout to Darvat. Don't kill me."

Since that time, Kumar Raza had kept his iron helmet on and the threat to Walinash's life constant, even when they'd landed twice in Maran to rest. He pushed the Naga and dragon to travel as fast as possible, worried the whole time he wouldn't arrive in Darvat soon enough to save Kanvar, wondering what sort of a trap his grandson had fallen into. Now they were crossing the last stretch of water toward Huayna, the capital of Darvat.

"Stay high over the city out of crossbow range," Kumar Raza ordered. "I won't have you controlling those humans down there, telling them to shoot me."

"I'm not that stupid," Walinash said through gritted teeth. "Their bolts would hit Brisbian before you. Where exactly do you want us to land?"

"Fly up the river. Do you feel any other Nagas?" Kumar asked.

"Do you think I'd tell you if I did? Lord Theodoric should never have trusted you."

"Lord Theodoric came here to save King Amar and fight in his behalf. By going against Amar, you betray your Lord and your King."

"Khalid is the rightful king. I serve him."

"King Khalid has been dead a thousand years. He has no right to steal another Naga's body to return unnaturally from the grave. Besides, you have no honor, you serve only yourself. You sided with Khalid because you thought doing so would bring you power and wealth. Faced with death, you even betrayed *him* to save your own sorry hide."

"You cannot blame a man for wishing to stay alive."

"No, but I can count on you to stay true to protecting your own welfare, so unless you want to feel my blade burn through your sorry skin, you'd better tell me exactly what Nagas you sense, how many, where they are, and what they are doing." Kumar Raza tightened his grip so his sword cut Walinash once more, not too much, not too deep, just enough to scare the wretched man into doing as he was told.

Walinash shivered. "Two of the Elite Naga Guardsmen, Bendyn and Weston, are in Huayna and have taken command of the city as King Khalid ordered. I don't sense anyone else."

"If you *think* one word to Bendyn and Weston, I will know it and kill you instantly. Do you understand?" Kumar Raza let his blade slice a fraction into Walinash's flesh. "Lord Theodoric has to be here somewhere, and Kanvar. Find them."

Walinash tensed. His heart beat so hard, Kumar Raza could feel it as he held the Naga in his grip. "I can't feel them," Walinash said. "Perhaps they're dead."

Kumar Raza ground his teeth. "You are such a liar. Kanvar and Theodoric are not dead." He refused to even think it. If he weren't wearing the helmet, he would be able to reach out to Kanvar's mind himself. Taking it off would be dangerous, but it was a risk he'd have to take. He slid the helmet from his head and snapped it down over Walinash's.

Walinash screamed, and his dragon trumpeted.

Kumar Raza ordered Brisbian to fly higher, hoping the distance coupled with Kumar Raza's feeble powers would keep the two Nagas on the ground from sensing him.

Kanvar, he screamed. *Lord Theodoric*. He hoped Kanvar and Theodoric would sense his call and make contact somehow.

As soon as he opened his mind up to find Kanvar and Theodoric, Bendyn sensed him. Grunting in annoyance, Kumar Raza tore the helmet off of Walinash's head and returned it to his own.

"Tell Brisbian to fly faster along the river up into the mountains," he ordered Walinash.

"Running won't do any good," Walinash said. "If the Naga Guardsmen have sensed you, they'll come for you. You won't have a chance."

"They can't feel me now, and you had better keep your mind locked away from them so they don't find us. If they come, they will die, and so will you. You can be sure of that. I am the Great Dragon Hunter. Three Nagas and three measly gold dragons are nothing to me. You saw what I did at the Maran Colony. You know what my spears can do. Do not call them, Walinash, or I won't spare them or you."

Walinash sucked in a breath of fear. He shook in Kumar Raza's grip, too frozen by Kumar Raza's threat to dare attempting to speak to the Naga Guardsmen below. Brisbian turned away from the city, following the river, flying high into the mountains.

A streak of gold flashed across the sky toward them.

"I warned you," Kumar Raza said, cutting Walinash deeper.

"I didn't. I swear by the fountain, I didn't call them. My mind is shielded."

Kumar Raza grabbed one of the spears off his back with his left hand as the gold dragon rushed to meet them, a Naga tucked neatly on its neck.

"Raza," Lord Theodoric's voice called out. "Ease up with the sword, you'll kill him."

Kumar Raza blinked at the Naga on the other dragon. It was Lord Theodoric that rode the ripple of gold that was the dragon in flight.

"He knows too much. He's trying to contact Khalid's Nagas below. I can't let him," Kumar Raza called out. Yes, Walinash knew about the helmet. In using it against him,

Kumar Raza had exposed Walinash to the knowledge of its existence. There was too much at stake to let the man live if he could give away their surprise weapon to Khalid's men.

"It's all right," Lord Theodoric said. "Lower your sword. I've got his mind shielded. But I can't feel yours. Why?"

"No, you can't. Whose side are you on?" Kumar Raza felt a moment of panic. If Lord Theodoric had changed sides, all would be lost. "Where's Kanvar?" Perhaps it had been Theodoric himself who had lured Kanvar into a trap.

"Kanvar's safe on the ground in hiding as King Amar ordered. I'll take you to him."

Kumar Raza bit back his panic and forced himself into a state of calm. Perhaps Lord Theodoric was telling the truth. Perhaps he was lying, attempting to draw Kumar Raza into the same trap that had stopped Kanvar. Either way, Kumar Raza had to risk going along with it. The only other choice was to kill Lord Theodoric and Walinash, and if he did that, he was far enough off the ground he would die with them. Better to land and then fight.

Kumar eased the sword from Walinash's neck.

Swearing bitterly, Walinash pulled out a vial of Great dragon saliva and spread it over the wound. Lord Theodoric's dragon winged away from the river and far out into the jagged teeth-like mountains, leaving behind all human habitations, and spiraling down toward the dense mountain wilderness. He landed beside a stream of water where boulders had cascaded across it to form a little pond. Lord

Theodoric's dragon folded its wings as Brisbian settled down beside them.

"Lieutenant, are you all right?" Lord Theodoric asked Walinash.

Kumar Raza jerked himself out from between Brisbian's plates and slid down his shoulder to the ground. With the earth firmly beneath his boots, Kumar Raza readied his spear and sword to strike at the dragons and Nagas. "Where is Kanvar?"

"Here, Grandfather." Kanvar limped along a narrow footpath that came down through the trees to the pool. "Grandfather?" he reached a hand toward Kumar Raza's forehead, but his touch was stopped by the helmet that incased it. "I can't feel you. It's like you're dead." He shuddered.

Kumar Raza grimaced and pointed his spear toward Lord Theodoric before giving Kanvar an explanation. "Do you trust him, with your life, with your soul, with the safety of every human living in this world?"

Kanvar glanced over at Lord Theodoric for a moment then back at Kumar Raza. "I trust him, Grandfather. We have no better ally."

Letting out a relieved breath, Kumar Raza sheathed his weapons. "Your last message was cryptic, 'It's a trap.' I feared one set by His Lordship. I am relieved to see you alive and well. What happened?"

"Come up to the house and I'll tell you," Kanvar said. "And I hope you'll tell me how you're shielding yourself so completely that it feels like you no longer exist. I'd blame a singing stone, but I hear nothing."

Kumar Raza hesitated, waiting while Lord Theodoric and Walinash dismounted from their dragons and started up the path ahead of them. When they were out of earshot, Kumar Raza tapped the side of his helmet. "Better than a singing stone, Kanvar. It's an iron box." He pulled the helmet off his head and shook out his sweaty hair. "Actually, I hate wearing it. It's very uncomfortable not being able to sense anything. Though General Chandran doesn't seem to have that problem with it at all."

Kanvar's brow furrowed. "Well, he's human. He never senses anything. So . . . an iron helmet?"

"Karishi's doing. He knows his metals, it seems."

Kanvar reached out with his good hand and lifted the helmet from Kumar Raza's grip. "Father said you'd found something." He hefted it as if trying to get a feel for its significance. "I'm glad because I . . . couldn't get the singing stones. I'm sorry, we cannot use them. Don't be angry. I know you need them, but I talked to Father, and he agrees. I have touched the stones and spoken with the ancestors. We must leave them in peace."

Kumar Raza's heart sank. "We need those stones, Kanvar. The helmets will be useful for keeping our own men free from Khalid's Nagas, but without the stones we can't free the Maran and Varnan armies from Khalid's command. If we can't free them, we'll have to fight them, and that will take an army larger than this world has ever known."

Kanvar took a step back and shook his head. "Then we are doomed. I cannot, will not, disturb the spirits of the dead." His eyes grew round with the same fear and resolve Kumar Raza had seen in Raahi's eyes when the Darvati boy had fought so desperately to make his way home to protect the spirits of his ancestors. Kanvar's eyes also held the same unbendable insistence Karishi had maintained when he'd said all singing stones had to be returned to Stonefountain. A finger of cold caressed Kumar Raza's spine. Those who had been touched by the dead were never the same again. He thought of Devaj and his encounter with Khalid at Stonefountain. The hair on Kumar Raza's arms prickled.

"All right, Kanvar. I can see I won't be able to change your mind about this." Kumar Raza grabbed the helmet back from Kanvar, tucked it under his arm, and strode up the path Lord Theodoric and Walinash had taken.

Kanvar clenched his fist as he watched Kumar Raza stalk away. His grandfather was taking this far worse than his father had. Kanvar frowned at the helmet. When Kumar Raza had taken it off, Kanvar had seen in his mind how difficult Walinash had made the journey. Kanvar's father had trusted the Naga's oath, but Kumar Raza truly believed Walinash was a traitor and a threat. The helmets must remain a secret, and Lord Theodoric and Walinash could blow their secrecy away with a single thought to one of the other Nagas anywhere in the world. Kumar Raza wanted helmets on both of them immediately and permanently until Stonefountain could be overthrown. Kanvar shuddered. The thought of having his mind locked inside one of those helmets choked him. Kanvar couldn't let his grandfather do that to Lord Theodoric, Walinash, or LaShawn.

Kanvar rubbed his head. *Father?* His father was far away, and without the aid of the spirits in the Hall of Raahi's Ancestors, Kanvar had a hard time finding him. Dharanidhar's mind was closer. He was headed toward Darvat across the Great North and bringing others with him.

What's wrong, Kanvar? Dharanidhar questioned. He was tired, his wing ached, and Kivi kept almost falling asleep. Since Dharanidhar relied on Kivi's eyes to see, he was most vexed at the lesser green serpent.

Wake up, Kivi! Kanvar shouted into the lesser serpent's mind.

Kivi yawned and stretched. *Hungry, food, too cold, must sleep*, the impressions came back to Kanvar.

Maybe going the northern way wasn't such a good idea, Kanvar said to Dharanidhar.

The northern way is the only way I could fly it.

Use Frost's eyes. She's not falling into hibernation up there. Kanvar could feel Frost's utter delight at returning to her natural home.

Dharanidhar chuckled. *True, she is enjoying herself. I used to be able to fly like that once, when I was young. But you were worried?*

I need to talk to my father, and I can't reach him. Kumar Raza is very angry with me, and I think I'm going to have to go argue with him. I don't want to do it.

Do what you have to do, Kanvar. I'll be there soon. I hate to miss a good argument.

Kanvar smiled grimly and limped up the trail to LaShawn's sorry excuse for a home. Raised voices came from inside.

"Put the spear down, Raza," Lord Theodoric ordered.

"Not a chance," Kumar Raza said.

Kanvar pushed into the room and found LaShawn bleeding from a spear scratch across his chest. Both Theodoric and Walinash had their swords out. Kumar Raza's sword lay on the floor between them as if he'd been forced to drop it. The helmet was back on his head, the visor down so Kanvar could only see his angry eyes through the slits. Kanvar had never realized his grandfather had a violently desperate side to him. But so much had happened: Khalid had risen again, the world had changed. Obviously, LaShawn had attempted to take control of Kumar Raza's mind, and Kumar Raza had responded decisively. Raahi sat next to the fire pit, his face still blank despite Kanvar and Theodoric's best efforts to restore his mind.

"Stop it, all of you." Kanvar slammed the door shut behind him.

Everyone remained as they were except for LaShawn who reached for Kumar Raza's sword.

"Stop! I order you to stop!" Kanvar shouted.

LaShawn glared at him and snatched up the sword.

"Lord Theodoric, did my father not give you a direct command to follow my orders?" Kanvar limped over to stand in between the three Nagas and his grandfather.

"Yes, he did," Lord Theodoric said through gritted teeth. "But I won't stand aside and let anyone attack my son."

LaShawn flushed with shame and his eyes dropped to the stump of the knees he stood on. He felt that if he were a real man, he wouldn't need his father's help in fighting Kumar Raza.

Kanvar laughed, even as his eyes stung with unshed, bitter tears. "LaShawn, twenty men couldn't defeat my grandfather in battle, and you three are only a heartbeat away from dying. Put the swords down now. In the name of King Amar, I command you, stop this fighting."

Lord Theodoric glared at Kumar Raza. "Tell him to put the spear down first."

Kanvar limped a step toward Kumar Raza and put his hand on the spear. "Grandfather."

"You need to listen to me, Kanvar," Kumar Raza said.

"I am listening to you. I saw what you were thinking, and I know what you fear, but I need you to trust me."

"I trust you, not them."

"Give me the spear." Kanvar pulled the spear gently but firmly out of his grandfather's hands.

"Twenty men might be a bit of an exaggeration," Kumar Raza said in a low voice as he surrendered his weapon to Kanvar.

"But you could have handled these three easily," Kanvar said loud enough everyone in the room would hear and understand.

"No question there," Kumar Raza said, squaring his shoulders. "The question is, should I have killed them while I had the chance? There is too much at stake here, and it will be far too easy for these men to betray us. Walinash for certain is a traitor."

"Lieutenant Walinash is an honorable man." LaShawn lifted the sword and advanced on Kanvar and Kumar Raza.

Kanvar leveled the spear at him. "Put the sword down, now. All three of you, or I give this spear back to my grandfather and lose three of my best men."

"You really think one human could defeat us?" LaShawn said.

"Can you feel his mind?" Kanvar asked. "Can you control him?"

LaShawn's brow furrowed as he tried to break into Kumar Raza's mind.

"No you can't," Kanvar said. "And because you can't, he could kill you. Even if you were unhurt and at your best fighting strength, he could kill you. The humans do not call him the Great Dragon Hunter for no reason."

Walinash choked, and Kanvar realized Walinash's face was white. His hand shook on the sword hilt. His mind tumbled with fear of Kumar Raza and . . . the other one, the blood monster, the red dragon. Kanvar caught the vivid memory of Rajan ripping one of the Naga Guardsmen to pieces with some sort of claws, biting and tearing with his teeth at the same time, roaring like a blood-lusted dragon.

"By the fountain," Kanvar whispered.

Having seen the same image, Lord Theodoric lowered his sword.

"You should have executed Rajan while you had the chance," Walinash said in a tight voice, and Kanvar realized, through the memories of the two Nagas, that Rajan had given himself over for execution to save Kumar Raza's life, and in exchange, Kumar Raza had saved Rajan's. The two brothers together were the most frightening pair of individuals in the world, except maybe Kanvar and Dharanidhar. Kanvar bared his teeth. In the back of Kanvar's mind, Dharanidhar roared in agreement.

Kanvar swung the shaft of the spear in an arc, slamming it against Walinash's, Theodoric's, and LaShawn's wrists in one hard strike, knocking the swords from their hands. "Swear fealty to King Amar now, or die," he told them, pressing the tip of the spear to Walinash's chest.

Outside, three gold dragons roared in anger.

"Careful," Kumar Raza said in a low voice. "Wounds from that spear cannot be healed by Great dragon saliva."

Kanvar's sweating hand tensed on the spear. "How can that be?"

Kumar Raza grinned. "Magic."

Kanvar turned his attention back to Walinash, pressing the tip of the spear even more firmly against the Naga's flesh. "Swear fealty to my father."

"I have already given King Amar my oath," Walinash said.

"Kumar Raza believes you have broken that oath, that you never intended to keep it," Kanvar said. "I'm sorry, Walinash, I must have your whole heart and soul in this. A traitor under any law is sentenced to death. But I don't want to kill you. I need men like you, true and honorable men, men who cannot be swayed by the lust for power and riches. Men whose hearts yearn for peace, but who have the courage to stand against evil and fight for it. Where do you stand, Walinash? Khalid is evil. He cares for no man but himself. He kills the innocent and tortures and enslaves the living. He uses his power to subdue the world to his will. My father is a man of peace who uses his powers in service to others, to lift and to heal, to bind together hearts that have been broken." Kanvar's voice faltered, caught behind the knot in his throat for a moment before he could speak again. "I know Kumar Raza would see you dead for your betrayal. But I also know my father would give you another chance. I'm giving you that chance, swear yourself to King Amar and mean it or—"

"Or what? You kill me? What kind of a choice is that?" Walinash said.

Kanvar lifted the spear away from Walinash's heart. "Let's forget for a moment everything that has happened before now. I will give you a free choice with one stipulation. You may swear fealty to King Amar and mean it with all your heart and soul, never to betray him again. Or you may go free, wherever you like, to serve whomever you will."

Walinash took a deep breath. A bit of color returned to his pale face. "What stipulation."

"If you choose to walk away free from this place and desert your king, I'll erase your memories and your dragon's memories of everything that happened from the attack on the Maran Colony until now. You will be left with nothing that can be used against us, but you will be free. It is what my father would insist on." Kanvar handed the spear back to Kumar Raza. "The choice is the same for all three of you. My father would only work with those who will give their hearts to him willingly. You are free, and no harm will come to you at his hand. You see, that is the difference between King Amar and King Khalid. Choose then, whom will you serve?"

Kanvar took a deep breath and waited. The small, one-room cabin fell silent.

"Kanvar?" a quiet voice by the fire whispered into the silence.

Kanvar snapped his attention to Raahi. His friend stood, looking around him in confusion. "Where am I? How did I get here?" His face flushed and he jabbed an angry finger at Kanvar. "You, you are going to take the stones. I have to stop you."

"Raahi." Kanvar limped over and took Raahi's hand, letting a wave of reassurance wash over Raahi's mind. "I asked you for the stones, but I was wrong to do it. I have spoken to your ancestors and left them in peace. The Hall is safe. The mountain is closed. I swear to you, I disturbed nothing. Ask them. I know you can speak to them even now. Ask them, and they will tell you. I have not betrayed your trust."

Raahi's eyes widened and grew unfocused for a moment. He let out a long sigh and sank to the ground beside the crackling fire.

Kumar Raza cleared his throat. "That was sweet, but a ridiculous distraction at a crucial moment. Kanvar has given you a choice, Walinash. I know Amar well enough to know it is what he would have given you. Well, what is your answer?"

Lord Theodoric dropped to one knee. "I have given King Amar my oath of service and do so again now willingly. He is the rightful king of Stonefountain, and I will serve him to the death. You need not fear any betrayal from me, Kumar Raza. Just, please, don't hurt my son. He's had more than his share of hurt already."

"If LaShawn fights me or tries to take control of my mind again, I will defend myself. I will kill anyone who attempts to betray our secrets to Khalid." Kumar Raza cast a dark look at LaShawn, whose chest still bled from the spear cut. The skin around the scratch had turned black and sickly. Kanvar retrieved the cup of dragon saliva he'd used to heal LaShawn's arm and spread saliva on the wound. LaShawn winced at Kanvar's touch, but the scratch remained open and bleeding.

"I told you that won't work," Kumar Raza said.

Kanvar narrowed his eyes at the spear. His grandfather, it seemed, had discovered some very effective ways of dealing with Nagas. It made Kanvar edgy, but he put a hand on LaShawn's shoulder and tried to ignore his grandfather, the helmet, and the spear. "I'm sorry he cut you. I know you wanted to live here in solitude and peace, and we have invaded your home. It is a sorry payment for your saving my life. We will fly from here the moment my dragon arrives. In fact, there is no need for Kumar Raza, Raahi, or I to spend the night in your house. We will camp out in the forest and leave you in peace. But before I go, I must have your decision. Too much is at stake for me to leave without it."

LaShawn frowned and turned away. He limped over to his mattress on the floor, sat down, and bowed his head. "I swear my oath of loyalty to King Amar, if I could serve him, I would, but I am nothing, not even a man. Go, and leave me in peace."

Kanvar nodded, and turned his attention to Walinash who had edged over to the door. "What is your choice?"

"You are all crazy," he said aloud while at the same moment screaming with his mind, *King Khalid, they have weapons they can use—*

The spear slammed into his chest, pinning him against the door, killing him instantly.

"No!" Kanvar yelled, too late. He rounded on Kumar Raza. "What have you done? We told him he could go free!"

"With a stipulation, which he knowingly tried to circumvent. He was spying for Khalid, Kanvar, and would have been our undoing." Kumar Raza strode over, pulled the spear free from the body, letting it slump to the ground.

"You were wearing the helmet; you could not have known he was calling for Khalid," Kanvar said. "You killed him in cold blood." Kanvar's chest hurt. As with all the deaths he had caused and witnessed, he'd felt the loss of the Naga's spirit as it tore free from his body and went to dwell wherever it was his ancestors gathered in death—Raahi's Hall, Stonefountain, some unknown chamber in Navgarod? Kanvar could not say. All he knew was the pain of Walinash's departure.

Kumar Raza pulled a cloth from one of his pouches and cleaned the head of the spear. "It was not murder, Kanvar. I know what he was doing. I could see it in his eyes. He was betraying us to Khalid. Do you deny it?" From another pouch he produced clean bandages and offered them to LaShawn, who took them with an angry glare.

Kanvar couldn't bring himself to say anything.

"Lord Theodoric, am I right?" Kumar Raza turned to the stunned Naga lord.

Theodoric blinked. "He was trying to tell Khalid about the spear. I assured you I would keep his mind shielded, but I wavered in that duty, distracted when you attacked my son. You would not have needed to kill him if I'd kept his mind bound." Guilt and sorrow twisted Theodoric's face.

"He tried to tell Khalid about the spear. What about the helmet?" Kumar Raza asked.

"The helmet?" Lord Theodoric said. "I don't understand."

"Listen, My Lord. I need to know exactly what Walinash said, word for word. Tell me."

Lord Theodoric repeated Walinash's treacherous call.

Kumar Raza grimaced, picked up his sword from where it had fallen, and sheathed it. "He said *weapons*, let's hope that is vague enough Khalid can do nothing with it." Kumar Raza got a hold of Walinash's body and dragged it out of the house.

"I'm sorry," Kanvar said to Lord Theodoric. "I know he was one of your men. A good man, I'm sure."

Lord Theodoric's face turned hard, and he looked away.

"Walinash and I were friends," LaShawn choked.

Raahi grabbed a cloth and water and set about cleaning up the blood by the door. Kanvar gave him a weak smile, glad that his friend's mind had returned. After helping Raahi clean up the mess, Kanvar stepped outside and stared across the sky, anxious for Dharanidhar to come.

Chapter Seven

Chains rattled above Aadi's head as the Maran schooner dropped anchor. Aadi came up out of a half-sleep into a crouch. The ever-present smell of salt water and wet wood greeted him, along with muffled footsteps from the deck above. Aadi climbed out of the cargo hold, straining to hear the sound of voices and the snap of the sails in the wind. All was silent. He passed the door to General Chandran's cabin and climbed out onto the main deck. A cold mist and the darkness of the dead of night surrounded him. There were men on deck, lots of them. No one spoke as two longboats were hoisted over the side and let down into the water.

Indumauli, Aadi called. *We've stopped moving. Where are we?*

Indumauli surfaced and sniffed the damp air. *I smell land. I think we may have come into the strait between Maran and*

Varna, the impression came from Indumauli's mind. Aadi pulled back behind a barrel as Qadim and his dragon hunters crossed the deck and started down to the boats. General Chandran clasped Qadim's arm in farewell without saying a word.

Aadi, Indumauli said, *if you want off the boat, I think you better leave it now. The dragon hunters are Varnans. That means we must be near the Varnan shore. This may be the closest you're going to get before General Chandran takes the ship to Maran.*

All right, I'm coming. Aadi leaned over to the edge of the boat. In the uncanny silence, if he jumped into the dark water below, it would surely make a splash that would alert General Chandran. He couldn't go down the ropes the dragon hunters were using without being seen.

Hurry, Indumauli said. *They're almost ready to cast off.*

Aadi glanced around, looking for a coil of rope through the misty night. He almost stumbled over one before seeing it. He tied an end to the railing and eased the length into the water. Then he slid down it into the cold waves. Indumauli's coils wrapped around him, and they shot toward shore, leaving behind the dragon hunters, the ghostly boat, and General Chandran. A few minutes later, Indumauli set Aadi down on a rocky beach and shook himself.

What I wouldn't give for some fresh water. Indumauli licked his lips.

Aadi rubbed a hand down the serpent's salt-crusted scales. "You don't look so good, Indumauli."

Indumauli slumped to the ground and moaned. *I never want to swim in the ocean again.*

"You'll have to. You can't stay on land. You have to at least swim along the shore until you find a river."

The one that leads to Stonefountain would be nice.

"That's a long way from here if we're in the channel by Daro." Aadi pictured a map of the world in his mind. "A long way. I can't go that far with you, I'll die. I have to get to Stonefountain the fastest way. I'll have to go on foot across the grasslands." Aadi knelt down beside the Great Black serpent. "Indumauli, tell me you're going to be all right."

Indumauli hissed and broke into a thirsty pant. *You go straight to Stonefountain. I'll make my way along the coast. Rivers flow to the ocean. I'll find them and rest in fresh water as I go. I'll meet you at Stonefountain. Don't worry, I may be uncomfortable, but I'm not dead yet. At least we made it across the ocean thanks to General Chandran.*

Aadi frowned and dug at the rocks. "I don't like General Chandran. He pretends to be working for King Amar, but I don't think he is."

I'm pretty sure he's working against Khalid one way or another. Indumauli got to his feet and shook himself. *I can't stay here, Aadi. I would spend the night with you if I could, but I have to find fresh water. I think I smell some close by.*

"Be careful of the humans," Aadi said. "Parmver told me there are far more here than in Kundiland, thousands of them, tens of thousands of them. I can't imagine it. I tried to make ten thousand checkmarks with my quill once. It took forever and I got bored and gave it up around three thousand."

Indumauli let out a hissing laugh and slithered back into the cresting waves. *You be careful too. I'll see you at Stonefountain.*

Aadi climbed up past the tide line and settled down to wait for dawn. He would only get himself lost stumbling about in the misty darkness in a land he'd never been to before. Dawn took its time in coming, growing lighter so gradually Aadi hardly noticed it through the mist. Then a salt breeze kicked up and swept the fog away. The sun laughed at him from its perch in the sky. Aadi got to his feet, shaded his eyes, and looked out across the land he'd come to. He saw buildings everywhere, made out of tan bricks that looked like nothing more than baked mud. They stood in clumps that grew bigger and closer together the farther east he looked, until a vast city filled the skyline.

"Daro," Aadi murmured. It had to be. Smoke from morning cook fires filled the sky. Clothing strung on lines from window to window flapped in the breeze. People bustled about everywhere, reducing Aadi's quill checkmarks to nothing more than itchekin scratches. Sunlight rippled over the city as a flight of Great Gold dragons passed overhead. Aadi gasped. Every dragon was ridden by a Naga, a full dozen of them. His first thought was to wave his arms and shout for joy, calling to them with his mind.

They were Nagas on magnificent gold dragons, flying proud and free. I've come home, Aadi thought. This is how the world should be.

Aadi. Indumauli sent urgent caution into his mind. *These Nagas are King Amar's enemies. They will most likely harm you, or worse, take you to Khalid. You told me you were going to sneak into Stonefountain undiscovered. You told General Chandran you had no intention of joining Khalid.*

Aadi's eyes stung. *But look at them. This is what the world must have been like a thousand years ago, before all the Nagas were murdered.*

That is no doubt the picture Khalid painted for Rajahansa, Indumauli said, *and look what happened to him. Do not try to talk to those Nagas, Aadi. I have trusted you. I have helped you. Do not betray my trust.*

Aadi swallowed hard and wrapped his arms around himself. Indumauli was the only friend he had at the moment. He did not want to anger the serpent. He forced his feet to carry him up off the beach and toward the city. Aadi's clothes dried quickly in the heat from the risen sun. His path took him first along the docks where dozens of ships lay at anchor. More were coming and going than he cared to count. He turned his back on the water and made his way through the crowds. They jostled him, but didn't seem to notice his existence. Their minds splashed up against his from all directions.

"Shields, Aadi," he told himself, hearing Parmver's voice in the back of his mind. Parmver had drilled him at shields for so many years Aadi had grown dead-tired of the tedious repetition, but it served him now. Taking a deep breath, he snapped his shields in place, clearing his mind. When he found himself alone with his thoughts, he was indeed alone. So alone, so empty. The emptiness gnawed at his soul, tearing at his heart, pressing against his lungs, making it hard to breathe.

He gasped and let his shields down a little. At least feeling the people and lesser dragons that swirled around him was better than being so alone. Men and women in long cotton robes flapped past him. Aadi thought their clothing looked strange, but after a half an hour in the direct burn of the sun while he wandered the maze-like city streets, he thought better of his first impression. There were no jungle trees here, no golden palace to shelter him from the full wrath of the sunlight. The buildings that stretched in continuous walls from one street to the next trapped the heat and intensified it even more than when Aadi had been out on the open ocean. His lips and skin, used to the moist heat of the jungle, grew dry and chapped.

The raised voices of shop vendors filled the streets. Aadi stumbled through the swirl of people, amazed at the things he saw for sale: cloth of all kinds and colors, dragon hides worked into camdor saddles, clothing, and furniture, small lesser dragons rattling their cages, pots and pans and jewelry and spices. The babble of voices and the smell of people and lesser dragons filled the air.

Aadi kept moving, but the deeper he got into the city, the more disoriented he became. He knew there was a south gate somewhere, and a road beyond that would take him out onto the grasslands. It used to stretch broad and straight to Stonefountain, but Parmver said the old road across the savannas had fallen to dust and vanished long ago. Once Aadi got out beyond the little towns that huddled around Daro like itchekin hatchlings, he could expect a long expanse of open land. But first he had to find the gate.

"Excuse me." Aadi pushed his way through a crowd of people around a man who was selling fertilized camdor eggs. The man caught sight of Aadi, looked him over, and frowned. "Not from around here, are you. What jati do you belong to?"

"I . . ." Parmver had never taught him that word. "Jati?"

"Not from Varna at all." The man shook his head in disgust and motioned Aadi away.

"Wait," Aadi said. "Can you tell me how to get to the south gate?"

The man stabbed his finger down the street in the direction Aadi had been going and went back to selling his brood of eggs.

Aadi went that direction until the street ended in a square. A half dozen other streets led off from the outdoor market that crammed every inch of space. Aadi almost got trampled by a camdor and its rider as it raced past. He dived aside at the last moment and leaned up against the burning hot bricks of a building to catch his breath.

Once again, he fought through the crowd to ask a vendor for directions. Then he started off down another street. By noon his stomach grumbled with hunger, but he had nothing he could barter in trade for the many sizzling delights that he passed. In the palace, he'd never gone hungry. He stopped, panting in the merciless dry heat. Once again he was tempted to contact the Nagas. They wouldn't let him die of hunger with food all around him in this wretched city.

Once again Indumauli, his mind far away and faint now, urged Aadi to stay away from Khalid's Nagas. *Find a well, get some water, rest for a moment in the shade*, Indumauli's mind snaked through his. Aadi did as Indumauli directed, though the public well was crowded, and he had to fight his way to get to it. Alas, he had nothing to hold the water in to drink and had to settle for scooping handfuls out of the bucket as others drew it up.

Aadi drank all his stomach could hold, letting the water fill what space a good meal should have taken. Then he retreated against a wall where a thin sliver of shade blocked the sun from his face. By that time, Indumauli's mind had vanished from his.

A Great Gold dragon roar shook the square around the well, and everyone froze. The Great Gold dragon flapped down to land. With a cry of fear, the crowd scattered, running in terror from the Naga on the dragon's back. Aadi stayed where he was as a wall of people crowded past him. I should run, he thought, but couldn't bring himself to do it. Abruptly, the terrified people stopped running, turned to face the Naga, fell into organized rows, and walked back into the square. Aadi found himself drawn out with them, the Naga's mind wrapped around his own, suppressing his thoughts, and replacing them with the will of the Naga.

"You have been chosen for a glorious duty," the Naga called out to the crowd. "Go to the south gate and join the others I have chosen." The command wrapped itself like steel chains around Aadi's mind, and he marched with the rest of the group. Though he didn't know where the south gate was, the others did, and he found himself there within minutes.

A mass of several thousand people were gathered outside the gate. Two Nagas and their dragons flanked the gate, sifting through the mind of each man, woman, and child as they came through, and directing them into groups—camdor keepers, blacksmiths, stoneworkers, farmers, carpenters, all of them together with lines of wagons loaded with supplies necessary for every trade. Aadi focused his thoughts to give the impression he was only a simple boy out in the streets of Daro.

"Stop." A Naga command froze Aadi in place as he stepped through the gate. The Naga glared down at him from his dragon's back. "You're not Varnan. Where are you from? What trade do you belong to?" Aadi shielded everything in his mind about his time at the golden palace and King Amar, bringing to the forefront his memories of growing up in the jungle village.

"I'm from Kundiland," Aadi said, "and I'm a scribe. I can read and write and do numbers, bookkeeping and—"

"Silence."

The words caught in Aadi's throat at the command. The Naga raked through Aadi's mind for some proof that he really had the skills he claimed to have. Aadi let him see enough to prove his claim and kept the rest of his mind darkened.

"Over there." The Naga pointed to a group of distinguished looking older men. *Ah well, he looks too weak for ditch digging anyway.* Aadi caught the impression of the Naga's thought to his dragon.

Looks like an untouchable to me, the dragon responded.

Aadi ducked his head and hurried away, not wanting the Naga to discover he could sense the main ideas behind the communication between Naga and dragon. He longed to tell the Naga he could not only read current writing, but he also knew the ancient language of Stonefountain. Gritting his teeth, he kept his mouth shut and his mind shielded. He would not betray Indumauli's trust in him.

As the day passed, the crowd grew larger and more organized, and supplies continued to pour out of the city. At nightfall, dinner was cooked by the group that handled that trade and served by the ragged men and women others called untouchables.

Aadi accepted a bowl of soup and a crust of bread along with a flask of water. He sat down a few feet away from the other scribes. None of them had spoken to him yet. Though Aadi's clothes were much finer than the dirty rags worn by the untouchables, only a trained eye would notice that beneath the crusted salt on them from the ocean. Aadi tried to brush the salt away to reveal the fine fabric beneath.

The other scribes paid him no notice. They talked amongst themselves instead, their minds lit up by the glorious vision the Nagas had planted there. All this gathering, all the people and wealth of the city was going to rebuild Stonefountain. The most magnificent city ever to be built was going to be restored, and they had the honor of being a part of that. Most of these scribes had been busy all day, cataloging and organizing every supply cart that wheeled from the city. It was their job to track everything and make sure supplies were distributed correctly.

Their joy was infectious. If Aadi had not felt so empty inside he might have jumped up and shouted with the wonder of it. As he sensed the other people around him, he realized that all were overcome with the majesty of the project they'd been chosen to undertake. Aadi shook his head, trying to clear it. These Nagas plied their craft well, inspiring unmatched devotion to Stonefountain and King Khalid. After a brief struggle, Aadi gave up and let his mind join all the others. He'd become a part of something great, something he'd longed for all his life, the return of the power of Stonefountain.

Chapter Eight

Come morning, the great caravan moved out. The elder scribe caught hold of Aadi's arm as he walked beside one of the wagons filled with quills, ink, paper, and writing desks. "Can you really write, boy?" he asked Aadi.

"Of course," Aadi said. What a silly question. It wasn't like any of them could lie to the Nagas.

"Good. Run these orders up to the head of the weaver Jati, read them to him, make sure he understands, then come back with his response." The elder scribe pressed a rolled paper into Aadi's hand.

Aadi nodded and ran off. He spent the day absorbed in these endeavors, running up and down along the caravan, reading out the orders given to him and scribing supply requests to be delivered to Eashan, the elder scribe who ran everything and reported directly to the Nagas. Lunch was served on the move, dry bread and bovinder jerky. Aadi did not complain. He was glad to have any food at all, no matter how simple. He grew tired quickly though, running about in the hot sun, and was glad for the flask of water he'd been given and for the water wagons where he could refill it. His relentless duty as runner kept him too busy to agonize much over the emptiness that consumed him.

In late afternoon, Aadi paused in a run between the architects and stonemasons, doubling over to catch his breath. A gold dragon settled to the ground beside him, and Aadi stiffened, expecting a scolding from the Naga on its back. The Naga was Lord Taral, the one Eashan reported to, the Naga responsible for the organized movement of the caravan. The humans were required to call all the Nagas Lord, though Aadi knew Lord Theodoric was lord over them all, and King Khalid was above Theodoric.

"I'm sorry, My Lord," Aadi said, panting. He kept his head down, fearing to look into the Naga's eyes. Taral's partner, Naga Lord Fistas, had already had three men whipped who had tried to steal food from the supply wagons.

"Have you ever ridden a camdor?" Lord Taral asked.

"No, My Lord," Aadi said.

"I want you to learn tonight after we stop. Go to the camdor keepers, have them train you and give you a mount. You're too slow on foot. It's ridiculous." Naga and dragon returned to the air to watch over the movement of the humans on the ground.

Aadi breathed a sigh of relief and finished delivering his latest message. At nightfall, the caravan stopped and made camp. Empty grasslands stretched out all around them, dotted only by the occasional acacia trees and herds of lesser dragons. Aadi jumped as a trihorn lumbered to its feet close by and went to join its herd several yards off. The trihorns were bigger than most of the lesser dragons back home in Kundiland. Though they seemed peaceful enough, nibbling the grass and rubbing up against the other members of their herd, Aadi did not like to be so close to them. He retreated to the other side of the wagons and found Eashan.

"Sir," Aadi said. "His Lordship Taral has ordered me to acquire a camdor and learn to use it tonight. Can a person really learn to ride a camdor in one evening?"

Eashan looked dubious. "If Taral commands it, I guess you'll have to. Run on over to the camdor keepers. You can eat dinner with them."

Once again, Aadi ran, afraid to slacken his pace. In his mind, he could feel Taral watching him. Aadi did not slow until he'd reached the first group of camdor keepers. The camdor keepers were spread throughout the wagon train since camdors were used to pull the wagons. The keepers had been divided into groups overseeing twelve wagons each. With the wagons stopped, the keepers were unhooking the camdors and tying them out to graze. Aadi raced up to one of the keepers whom he'd brought orders to earlier in the day.

115

"Still have you running ragged?" the man said, leading a pair of camdors out with the others.

"The Naga, His Lordship Taral, has ordered me to learn to ride." Aadi breathed deeply to catch his breath. "I've never ridden a camdor before."

"Ever been around any?" The keeper patted the camdor's neck and strode off to a group of camdors staked out by the keepers' wagon, motioning for Aadi to follow.

"No sir. I'm a scribe. I'm good at writing. Not sure why they've turned me into a messenger. Isn't there a messenger jati or something?" After working all day with the jatis, Aadi had figured out the word meant trade skill group, though to the Varnans it carried deeper meaning. People from one jati did not eat or co-mingle with members of another. They worked together, but in their minds they were all separate classes.

The keeper grinned. "The messengers are busy carrying important messages, not supply requisitions. That requisition job has always fallen to the youngest of the scribes in a caravan. Though I daresay there has never been a caravan as big as this, so the young scribes haven't needed to be trained in camdor riding before."

The keeper stopped beside a tan camdor with black stripes like lightning on its sides. The camdor reared back as Aadi walked up to it.

"Sh." The keeper ran a calming hand down the camdor's front leg. "Easy there, girl."

The camdor snorted and settled down on her haunches.

"You have to move slow and easy around them, no sudden movements, keep your voice soft. They're skittish. This is Jenna. She's helped me train a lot of riders. Come over here slowly and put your hand out so she can smell you."

Aadi slowed his breathing, held his hand out, and inched toward the camdor. He felt Jenna's mind brush up against his own. She blinked sleepily. The sun had set. That meant rest time. She hated to run at night, though she'd done it in the past when the keepers made her. She sniffed Aadi's hand and snorted, not wanting anything to do with him after a long day.

I'm sorry, Aadi whispered into her mind, hoping she would understand the meaning behind his thought. He moved closer and rubbed a sore muscle along her side that was paining her. She lowered her head as he massaged away the ache.

The camdor keeper let out a low chuckle. "It seems she likes you."

"She's tired," Aadi said, "and her muscles are sore. Something must have happened today to hurt her."

The keeper drew Aadi away from the camdor. "She tripped. How could you know that?"

Aadi shrugged. "Her muscles are bunched tight where she's sore, and she's grumpy. I always get grumpy when I'm tired."

The keeper squeezed Aadi's shoulder. "I think you were born into the wrong jati, lad."

"I don't think that I should ride Jenna tonight, but I don't want Lord Taral to whip me for going against his commands either. Is there a different camdor I could use?"

The keeper frowned. "None as good natured and well trained for teaching new riders as Jenna. You might be a natural with the camdors, but riding them is not a skill that is easily mastered."

The keeper pulled a flask of liniment from his pocket and went back to Jenna. "Come on now, grumpy girl. You are not that hurt or that tired." He rubbed the liniment over the sore muscles and showed Aadi how to saddle and bridle the camdor.

Jenna rolled her eyes as she took the bit in her mouth. She snorted in annoyance as the keeper walked her away from the other camdors to a mounting block beside the wagon. "Now listen here, Jenna," the keeper said as he positioned her beside the block. "I need your help tonight. This young man could be seriously punished if he does not learn to ride. You need to show him the movements, help him get it right. Don't give him any trouble. If you're a good girl, I'll give you three apples when you're done."

Though the keeper spoke to Jenna as if she were a Great dragon and could understand his words, Aadi sensed Jenna's mind only recognized the tone of his voice. This was how the keeper always talked to her before letting stupid riders mount her who did unexpected things like turn the reins wrong or slip unexpectedly out of the saddle on sharp turns. Jenna steeled herself to comply. The keeper wanted her to be patient and move slowly. Jenna's mouth watered. The keeper always gave her a special treat when she handled the stupid humans correctly.

Aadi smiled and rubbed Jenna's shoulder.

The keeper gave him some simple directions on how to mount, sit, and guide the camdor. Aadi paid close attention. He did not want to make Jenna's life too difficult, especially since he was disturbing her rest. He got up on Jenna's back and tried to sit the correct way.

"Straighten your back," the keeper said. "Roll your hips forward a bit so your center of balance is in line with her back legs that are beneath you. Since camdors run upright on their hind legs, balance is very important. If I had time and someone a bit smaller than you with me, I'd make you carry him on your back so you can get the feel of it. Camdors are strong, but they have to work extra hard and can be injured if you throw them off balance."

Jenna's muscles tensed and she shifted on her back legs until Aadi got his seat balanced correctly. Then she relaxed.

"That's better," the keeper said. "Now take her around in a circle, out to the other camdors and back. Don't jerk the reins. Just move them in a fluid motion. Stay relaxed. The more you tense up, the harder time you'll have keeping your balance."

"All right, Jenna." Aadi eased the reins over to get her to turn out toward the grassland. As he did so, he sent a picture to her mind of where he wanted her to go.

Jenna let out a rumbling purr that tickled his legs where they pressed up against her sides. Then she loped away from the wagon. Aadi thought he'd been ready for her sudden movement, but it still caught him by surprise. He flew backward and only kept himself from falling by clinging to the reins. His sudden jerk on the reins brought Jenna to a stop. She huffed, reset her back legs, and waited for Aadi to regain his balance and sit back down right in the saddle. *I'm sorry, Jenna,* Aadi said. *I'm trying.*

Jenna lashed her long tail against the ground and set out once more, slower this time. *Stupid human.* She consoled herself by thinking about the keeper's treat that waited for her when she was done.

An hour later, the keeper let Aadi dismount. Every muscle in Aadi's body screamed in protest as his feet touched the ground and he tried to walk. He wavered, and Jenna pressed her shoulder against his chest to keep him from falling. "Thank you, Jenna," Aadi said. "I have never been so sore. Do you want me to unsaddle her?" he asked the keeper.

"Go ahead. She seems fond of you. I suppose I'll have to let you use her until we reach Stonefountain. But you'll have to take full responsibility for her care."

"Yes sir." Aadi had grown very fond of Jenna in their short time together as well. He eased the saddle off of her, looped the tie rope around her neck, unbuckled the bridle, and slid the bit out of her mouth.

The keeper brought over some apples and handed them to Aadi. "She likes these. Watch your fingers though; keep your hand flat." He explained to Aadi how to feed and care for Jenna.

Jenna purred as Aadi gave her the apples. *Stupid human listened to Jenna, watched Jenna, learned fast. Won't be stupid for long,* Jenna thought.

"My name is Aadi," Aadi said aloud. Then he spoke directly into Jenna's mind. *I don't want to be stupid. I want to be your friend.*

Stupid Aadi, give Jenna another treat, Jenna thought.

Aadi had already given her the last of the three apples. "May she have another one, please?" Aadi asked the keeper.

"One more, and only one more. She'll give herself a stomach ache if she eats too many." The keeper gave one more apple to Aadi, who presented it to Jenna.

Stupid Aadi, Jenna likes. Jenna gobbled the apple and rubbed her head against Aadi's chest.

The next morning Aadi started his work with enthusiasm. Though the sun shone on him just as hot as before, and he had to cover just as much distance back and forth along the caravan, he had a lot more fun. Within a few hours on Jenna's back, despite his protesting muscles, Aadi felt comfortable and confident riding the camdor. More than that, the sweeping emptiness inside him was swallowed up with Jenna's presence. As long as he was with her, touching her, riding her, he was not so alone. For Jenna's part, she had never had a keeper who understood her so well, who could get right inside her mind and run with her as if he were an extension of her own body. The two of them became fast friends.

Aadi found his joy and anticipation mounting as the caravan plodded its way across the grasslands toward Stonefountain. He'd studied so much about the ancient city, he could hardly believe he was going to see it in person. Lord Taral and the other Nagas swept by overhead often. Whenever Taral was around, Aadi sensed the Naga watching him, and Aadi worked hard to please him. But when Lord Fistas flew over, Aadi kept his head down and tried to stay out of sight. Fistas's presence was brooding and angry. He was in charge of keeping discipline in the caravan and hated the humans he'd been given charge over.

Aadi squeezed his eyes closed and pressed his head against Jenna's neck as Fistas's dragon snatched up a member of the farmer jati who had lagged far behind his group. The dragon roared and shook the man then flapped forward and dropped him among his peers. Another time, two humans tried to escape, sneaking off into the tall grass.

Fistas caught them and personally whipped them into unconsciousness.

But Lord Taral wasn't like that. He landed often to speak to the heads of the jatis to give them encouragement, laughing with them over small things he found humorous, seeing what they needed and giving instructions to Eashan to make sure their needs were filled.

In the late afternoon, while Jenna jogged back from the front of the caravan where Aadi had scribed a requisition for more water for the camel herding jati, a spineback raptor lunged out of the tall grass beside Jenna, intent on taking down a bovinder that had fallen back from the herd driven by the bovinder herding jati.

Jenna screamed and pivoted in fright, nearly unseating Aadi. A pair of dragon hunters that were acting as outriders for the caravan speared the raptor before it could sink its claws and teeth into the bovinder. Aadi tried to calm Jenna, but her instincts to race away from the predator blocked out his soothing thoughts. Still screaming, she got the bit between her teeth and raced away from the caravan, making sudden sharp turns as she ran. Aadi dropped the reins, leaned forward, and wrapped his arms around her neck to keep from being thrown off.

"Jenna, please, stop," he cried, but Jenna was beyond reason.

Hold your breath, Lord Taral's command burst into Aadi's mind, freezing his lungs. Taral's dragon flew past

Jenna and puffed sparkling joy breath in her face. Jenna sat down on her haunches and swayed back and forth, all thoughts of danger forgotten.

Aadi let go of Jenna, slid from her back, and stumbled away, his lungs screaming for air. He panicked, fearing suffocation, but Lord Taral released Aadi's lungs, letting him breathe. As Aadi caught his breath, Lord Taral and Lord Fistas landed in front of him.

Aadi dropped to his knees in terror. "Please, please don't whip me. I wasn't trying to escape. I swear by the fountain, I wasn't."

With a look of pure hatred, Lord Fistas dismounted and strode toward Aadi, but Lord Taral intercepted him with a firm hand against his chest. "The boy's mine, Fistas. I assure you, he was not trying to escape. The razor-back startled his camdor is all."

"Any messenger knows how to control a startled camdor," Fistas said.

"He just learned to ride last night. It's amazing he wasn't flung off and trampled. I've seen riders injured, even killed in situations like that. Lay off, Fistas. Let me handle the boy."

Lord Fistas cracked his whip so it stung Aadi's ear. "I'm watching you, boy. Don't think you'll get away with this a second time." He pivoted back to his dragon, and flew off.

A terrified sweat drenched Aadi, dripping salt into his eyes. He stayed on his knees, not daring to look up, not daring to move. He flinched as Lord Taral's hand touched his shoulder.

"It's all right, Aadi," Lord Taral said. "Get up now. Walk your camdor back to the scribe wagons and tell Eashan I've ordered you to take the rest of the day off. It's already late, and your camdor will be no good for riding for a while. Have the keeper look her over and make sure she's not hurt. I'll come and check on you after dinner."

Too frightened still to speak, Aadi stumbled over to Jenna, took hold of the reins, and led her back to the caravan. He found Eashan and managed to stutter out Lord Taral's orders.

Eashan frowned. "You're lucky to be alive. Camdor riding is for the messenger jati. They should assign me a real messenger so you don't have to do it."

"I . . . I like scribing the messages," Aadi said. A bleak fear went through him at the thought that he might be forced to give up Jenna. He needed her as badly as he needed air to breathe. She was the only thing holding off the emptiness that consumed him.

"Then you should walk from now on," Eashan said.

"No, please. I love riding. I can do it. It wasn't my fault the raptor attacked the caravan and spooked her." Aadi clenched Jenna's reins as if he would never let them go.

Eashan gave Aadi a dark look. "I will discuss this with Lord Taral, and we will both accept his decision no matter what it is. Now take that creature to the keeper, and don't you dare get back on her."

Aadi lowered his head and led Jenna away in despair. Jenna burbled along happily beside him, her head bobbing with pleasure until the joy breath wore off. Then she jerked up in surprise, nearly pulling the reins from Aadi's hands.

"Easy there," Aadi said, trying to calm her, but his own fear and sadness spooked her worse. She reared back and trumpeted, slashing the air with her claws. Aadi had to jump aside to keep from having a gash torn across his face. "Jenna, no, please. Please calm down. I'll give you apples."

Treats. Jenna stopped thrashing and cocked her head. *Aadi have treats?*

"We're going to get some from the keeper if you'll just come along quietly."

Jenna huffed, lowered her head, and let Aadi lead her to find the camdor keeper. In truth, it was the keeper who found them. He rode up, face flushed, and dismounted. "I heard what happened. Are you all right?"

Aadi nodded. "She's still kind of spooked, but I don't think she's hurt. I hope not. Eashan says I have to leave Jenna with you. He's going to try to convince Lord Taral not to let me ride anymore." Aadi could not keep the bitterness out of his voice. He did not want to leave Jenna's side. Lord Taral had said he could have the rest of the day off. That meant he could stay with Jenna and the keeper for now if he wanted to. Eashan might be furious, but Aadi did not care.

The camdor keeper rubbed Jenna's head and took hold of the bridle. "Well Jenna, looks like you're coming back with me."

Jenna jerked out of the keeper's grasp, twisted around, and slammed her tail into his gut. He doubled over with a grunt of pain. Jenna snorted and moved behind Aadi. The keeper gasped and straightened, staring in disbelief over Aadi's shoulder at Jenna.

"I-I didn't tell her to do that," Aadi said.

"Of course you didn't. How could you?" The keeper glared at Jenna for a moment then turned his attention to Aadi. "I guess she's staying with you . . . for now. Mount up and take her in a circle so I can see if she's hurt."

"I'm forbidden to ride."

"Walk her out then." The keeper led his own camdor out of the way and motioned for Aadi to take Jenna around.

"Come on Jenna." Aadi tried to lead Jenna out, but she sat back on her haunches and refused to move.

Treats, Jenna thought. *Find keeper, get treats.*

Aadi cleared his throat, embarrassed. "She wants an apple. I promised her I'd give her one if she calmed down and let me lead her."

"You've got to be kidding," the keeper said with a scowl. "Who's in control here, you or her?"

"I think she is," Aadi said.

"You have to teach them who is boss, Aadi. Be gentle but firm. The camdors will never respect you and obey your commands if you don't make them do what you want. Get hold of the reins up by the bridle, bring her head down, and walk her out."

"Take the reins near the bridle like you did?" Keeping an eye on Jenna's tail, Aadi slid his hand up to where the reins met the bit in Jenna's mouth.

The keeper chuckled. "Jenna doesn't usually act out like that, but she's had a hard day, and I was being rather abrupt. Just bring her head down gently and walk her out. She knows better than to try that again." The keeper eased a riding crop out from a loop on his belt.

Jenna snorted and shuffled her hind legs.

"Come on, Jenna." Aadi eased her head down. Jenna resisted him for a moment, but the keeper twitched the riding crop. Jenna let out a sigh, lowered her head, and started walking before Aadi even moved his feet. He had to two-step to catch up with her. They walked in a circle together and came back to the keeper.

"She's fine," the keeper said, tucking the crop back into his belt. "Take her to my wagon and get her an apple. I swear I've never seen a camdor impress on a rider so fast in my life, and never one like Jenna who has had hundreds of riders before. She'll carry anyone. At least she always has before." The keeper looked hard at Aadi for a moment.

"It's too bad you belong to the scribe jati. Once we reach Stonefountain, you'll be back at your books, and I'll have to train Jenna all over again to get her to accept other riders."

Frowning, the keeper mounted his own camdor and loped away.

"Well, Jenna," Aadi said. "Let's go find that apple."

Jenna purred in agreement and walked sedately beside Aadi to the keeper's wagon.

Chapter Nine

Aadi walked with Jenna beside the keeper's wagon until the caravan stopped for the night. Then he wiped her down with the oils used to keep her scales from cracking in the dry heat as the keeper had explained he must do each night. After that, he checked her teeth and claws and tied her out to feed. The camdors were omnivores. She chewed on the long grasses for a while then used her claws to tear up the ground and catch the field mice and lizards in their dens.

Aadi accepted a plate of baked beans from an untouchable that brought dinner around and ate his own meal while Jenna ate hers. He jumped to his feet when Lord Taral's dragon swooped down to land beside the wagon. Lord Taral dismounted and strode up to Aadi.

"My Lord," Aadi said, bowing. Surely Taral had spoken to Eashan by now, and Aadi was frightened to hear he must leave Jenna and never see her again.

Lord Taral narrowed his eyes at Aadi. "You're awfully fond of that camdor."

Aadi swallowed back his fear and kept his shields up around his mind, not wanting Taral to feel the desperate emptiness that devoured him. "Yes, My Lord. I know Elder Eashan does not want me to ride anymore, but I can do it. Jenna and I work well together."

Lord Taral laughed quietly. "Yes, you do." His brow furrowed. "That's the problem."

"That's a problem?" Aadi blurted out a bit more forcefully than appropriate in speaking to the Naga Lord. He bit his tongue and bowed his head, expecting a reprimand, consoling himself that someday he would be a Naga too and could speak out as he wished.

"You're not from Varna?" Lord Taral leaned against the wagon and stared out across the grasslands at the grazing trihorns.

"No, My Lord. I'm a native of Kundiland."

"Alas, this is not Kundiland." Lord Taral dropped his hand down to rest on the hilt of his sword and directed his gaze southwest toward Stonefountain. This is Varna, and the Varnans, it seems, have a strict class system. Scribes are not camdor riders. There is no fluidity between classes. You claimed to be a scribe and have been adopted into their jati. That means you can't be a camdor trainer, keeper, or message rider. Those jatis are below yours, and the other scribes are upset that I would ignore their class structure by ordering you to ride."

Aadi set aside his dinner, no longer hungry. So Eashan's objection to Aadi's riding wasn't about keeping him safe at all. "My Lord, where you are from, are there jatis?"

Lord Taral shook his head. "Aesir is a beautiful city. A peaceful city. A man may choose what profession he wishes to pursue. If he's good at it, he can rise to whatever prominence his endeavors can take him. And even as a very rich man, if he wishes to marry some beggar off the street, no one will stop him. The people of Aesir are free. I do not like this Varnan class system and hope King Khalid can prevail upon them to give it up once we rebuild Stonefountain."

Aadi stared at the ground and kept his shields up to guard his spinning mind. Lord Taral considered the people ruled by the Nagas as free and the Varnans as captives within their own class system. The irony puzzled Aadi.

"Is something bothering you?" Lord Taral asked. "Feel free to speak your mind. I won't harm you."

"You . . . you say the humans of your city are free, and yet you've just enslaved thousands of people in this caravan, binding their minds, forcing them to leave their homes in Daro against their will. Lord Fistas is whipping people close to death who try to escape." Aadi's voice cracked and he broke off speaking. Lord Taral had invited him to, but he probably shouldn't have said so much. He cringed, expecting punishment.

Lord Taral took hold of Aadi's arm and turned him to face him. "Aadi, look at me."

Aadi kept his head bowed. He was in real trouble now.

"Look at me." Lord Taral used his power in a gentle nudge of Aadi's mind to force his head up to look Taral in the eyes. Taral's blue eyes held a deep earnestness. "You cannot understand this now, but we are part of a great work. For a thousand years people on this side of the world have lived in darkness and poverty, scrabbling like kitrats in the mud, binding themselves to jatis, living in primitive houses. By the fountain, Aadi, how can we let these dark ages endure? It may seem hard for you now, but what we're doing is important. You may not understand, but it is only because you have no vision of the future. The people of this caravan will be lauded as heroes throughout the coming ages—the brave men and women who left their squabbling in the dirt to build a bright city, glorious, clean, and free. Stonefountain will once again be the jewel of the world, a place of learning, art, and culture. And you get to be a part of that, Aadi. We're not destroying this civilization; we're restoring it."

The glorious vision Lord Taral cast into Aadi's mind swallowed up his doubts and fears with wonder and joy. He knew he was lucky to be one of the chosen to go to Stonefountain. He was part of the greatest revival in a thousand years. But the empty darkness inside him would not recede completely before the bright vision of Stonefountain restored.

In a last effort of will, Aadi pulled free from Lord Taral and looked away. "K-Khalid is evil. Everyone knows he's an evil tyrant. How can you serve such a man?"

Lord Taral laughed. "Oh, Aadi. I do not believe His Majesty is as bad as your folklore makes him out to be. Those are just stories made up by your leaders to keep you in darkness, to keep all the power for themselves. They say King Khalid was evil, a king you never knew who lived a thousand years ago. And because King Khalid was evil, all Nagas are evil and must be killed. But you see, it has nothing to do with good or evil. It is just the human leaders who wish to keep their position and power over other humans. They spin stories to make people fear the Nagas, so they can keep their subjects' minds in darkness and locked in servitude to them. Look at these jatis. Don't you see it? The jati elders keep everyone in their place. Eashan does not want you to be free to ride a camdor, because he would no longer have complete control over you. When we get to Stonefountain, you will find that King Khalid is not the monster people make him out to be."

"But—"

"Do you think I'm evil, Aadi?"

Aadi shook his head. Lord Taral had been nice to him, he'd watched over him, given him Jenna, and saved his life when Jenna spooked. "But Lord Fistas."

"My brother is only doing the job he's been assigned. If some people were allowed to steal food or run away, it would hurt all the rest of you. If order isn't kept, the caravan would break apart in chaos. People would fight each other for food and water. Women and children could be trampled, or worse, lost alone out on the grasslands to be hunted and devoured by spine-back raptors. And you scribes, would be slaughtered since you have no basic skills in self defense and survival. Yes, some people suffer at my brother's hands. He has to make himself seem hard and cruel to keep the criminal elements of humanity in check. But he does it for the greater good of all." The red-gold rays of the setting sun illuminated Lord Taral's face.

"Lord Fistas is your brother?" Aadi whispered.

"Yes, and he's really not such a bad person once you get to know him."

If you're a Naga, Aadi thought to himself. He'd sensed Lord Fistas's mind and knew Fistas despised the humans. "Yes, My Lord," Aadi said out loud. "I think I understand. I feel honored to serve you and be a part of this great movement."

Lord Taral smiled. "I knew you had a sense of vision. I like how hard you work. I've never caught you slacking, never seen you doing anything but the business Eashan has assigned you. That's rare in someone your age. Most boys are not so dutiful. Because of that, I have told Eashan in no uncertain terms that you are to keep your camdor now and forever. I have bought her from the keeper and give her to you as a gift. So much for stupid Varnan jatis." He clapped Aadi on the back, mounted his dragon, and flew away.

Aadi cried out in joy.

Jenna jerked her head up in surprise.

"Jenna," Aadi said. "You're mine forever. Lord Taral just gave you to me." He spoke the words out loud and sent the impression of their meaning into her mind.

Power Lord gave Aadi treats? Jenna thought.

Aadi smiled. "Yes, Jenna. He did."

Kanvar climbed up the slope above the pool and shaded his eyes, watching the horizon for Dharanidhar. He could feel him close by. Finally, a dark sparkle of blue glinted as Dharanidhar flew around a jagged peak. Kanvar's heart leaped for joy as Dharanidhar settled the boat he carried on the water and landed on the ground beside the pool.

"Dhar!" Kanvar limped back down the rough slope, the rocks clattering beneath his boots as he half-slid to get to his friend. He wrapped his arms as far as they would go around one of Dharanidhar's forelegs and pressed his face against Dharanidhar's rough scales.

Kanvar. Let me have a look at you. Dharanidhar nudged Kanvar back and leaned his head down to Kanvar's level. Kivi, the lesser green serpent, was wrapped around Dharanidhar's head with its own head lying on top of Dharanidhar's dragonstone. The green serpent blinked contentedly at Kanvar. It was warm again and happy though a bit hungry and anxious for Dharanidhar to feed it.

Kanvar reached out and stroked the green serpent's back. "Greetings, Kivi."

With Dharanidhar's neck lowered, Karishi and Tazaran detached themselves and dropped to the ground beside Kanvar. Kanvar ignored them. It seemed like forever since he'd been with Dharanidhar, ever since the Naga Guardsmen had captured Kanvar in Kundiland and carried him off to Stonefountain.

"I'm so glad to see you," Kanvar said to Dharanidhar.

And I'm glad to see you, Dharanidhar rumbled.

Kanvar realized with a start that this was the first time Dharanidhar had ever gotten a full look at him. Kanvar had blinded Dharanidhar the moment they met, and Dharanidhar's only vision of the world since then had been through Kanvar's eyes. Until now. Now he had Kivi to see for him.

Kanvar took another step back and turned so Dharanidhar could look at him from all sides. "What do you think?"

Well, Dharanidhar grumbled, suppressing a laugh. *You are a cripple.*

Kanvar laughed. "As if you didn't know that."

Yes, I knew it, but I've never seen it before. Now I better understand the difficulty you have sometimes. Poor little crippled boy. Dharanidhar could not hold back his laughter any longer.

He let out a chortle of joy and flicked Kanvar backward into the water.

Kanvar thrashed his way up on shore and spit the water from his mouth. From inside the boat, Miki barked and Frost chortled. "Stop flapping, Frost," Denali cried. "You'll tip us over."

Ignoring them as well, Kanvar lifted a fist to Dharanidhar. "I may be crippled, but I'm not little or poor. I'm a prince, second heir to the throne of Stonefountain."

You're a cripple and a lousy dragon hunter. Dharanidhar opened his jaws so blue fire crackled between his teeth.

"At least I'm not old and blind," Kanvar said. Then both of them fell to laughing again. Kanvar laughed so hard his sides hurt and his eyes watered. Dharanidhar lit the sky above their heads with blue fire.

"Hey, cut the fire. We're supposed to be hiding here." Lord Theodoric stepped out from the trees where he'd been watching the exchange between Kanvar and Dharanidhar.

Dharanidhar snapped his jaws closed to douse the fire and looked over at Theodoric. *You,* he bared his teeth, s*tole Kanvar from me and left me to die stranded on a cliff, blind and alone.*

Lord Theodoric lifted a placating hand. "I was only following Devaj's orders because I thought King Amar was dead. I had no idea Khalid was controlling Devaj."

Denali paddled the boat to the edge of the pool and beached it. Miki jumped out and raced over to Lord Theodoric.

He sniffed Theodoric for a moment then lifted his leg on Theodoric's boots. Theodoric jumped back, just as Frost flashed her dragonstone at him. Sensing it coming, Denali put his hand over the dragon's stone to block the light.

Do you like the army I brought you, My Lord? Dharanidhar said. *A dog, a hatchling, and a boy. Khalid will have no chance against us.*

Lord Theodoric's mind tumbled into confusion, and Kanvar laughed. "He's joking, My Lord. Dharanidhar has an individual sense of humor."

Lord Theodoric looked up at the towering blue dragon, staring at the dragon's milky white eyes and scars-upon-scars across his body. "I've been told Great Blue dragons are very ferocious."

"Oh, he is that," Kanvar said. "Of course, so am I."

Tazeran hissed and pawed at the rocks on the ground.

"Sorry Taz, there's nothing but granite here," Kanvar said. "But there's a cave on the other side of this ravine, up behind LaShawn's house. You might find something worth eating there, but be careful; it's a Great Gold dragon's lair."

"Since when do Great Gold dragons make a lair in caves?" Karishi asked. "I thought they all lived in civilized dwellings: mansions and palaces and such."

Kanvar opened his mouth to explain, but Lord Theodoric cut him off.

"Who are you?" Theodoric asked Karishi. "Are you bound to that metal dragon?"

Tazeran hissed, flicking his tongue out at Theodoric. Karishi's copper armor rippled as he dropped his hand to the sword he wore at his side and drew it partway out.

"Wait, wait." Kanvar moved in between the two men and held his hand out. "Karishi, this is Lord Theodoric. I believe my father told you about him. My Lord, this is Karishi. He's your grandson."

Karishi let the sword slip back into its sheath. "Grand-father?" His mind was shielded, his emotions guarded so Kanvar couldn't sense them.

Lord Theodoric took a deep breath and forced himself to smile. His mind churned, unsure how he should react to the man who stood before him. Having been told by Kanvar about Karishi's abandonment as a child and all his many years growing up alone, Lord Theodoric had ex-pected a skinny, wilted man, with timid eyes. But Karishi was no-thing like Theodoric had pictured. Karishi was tall and strong and as muscled as any Darvati blacksmith. His exquisite ar-mor glinted in the sun, matching the spark of fire in his eyes. Karishi was as impressive as any Naga Lord in Aesir, in truth, more impressive than most. His austere life had not reduced him to a wasted man like it had his father.

"I'm honored to meet you, Karishi." Lord Theodoric stepped forward and held an arm out in greeting.

Still guarded, Karishi clasped it. "And I, you."

Kanvar let out a relieved breath. He knew how lonely Karishi had been and wanted him to get along with his family.

"Hey, there's a house up there." Denali had gone partway up the path and returned. "Looks like a tribal longhouse, only not quite so long. It's a terrific place, if you can stand a permanent dwelling. I didn't know there were any of my people in Darvat."

"A terrific place?" Lord Theodoric said in disbelief.

"Denali's from the Great North," Kanvar explained. "The people of his tribe live in tents made from animal hides. LaShawn's fieldstone house is practically a mansion compared to that."

"It's one room, with a dirt floor, and a fire pit," Lord Theodoric said, frowning.

"Sounds perfect. Let's go," Denali said.

"Wait, Denali." Kanvar motioned for him to come back. Denali jogged over to Kanvar, with Miki and Frost at his heals. "That's LaShawn's house. He doesn't like visitors. I mean *really* doesn't like visitors. Our camp is that way, over in the trees. Why don't you go start a fire then come back to the river and catch us some fish for dinner. The only person going to visit LaShawn right now is Karishi."

"Why?" Denali put his hands on his hips.

"Because LaShawn is Karishi's father," Kanvar said.

Denali dropped his arms to his sides. "Where's my father?"

"Kumar Raza has gone to the villages to recruit blacksmiths to make iron helmets. We're going to need thousands of them." Kanvar frowned at the impossibility of putting together an army large enough to take Stone-fountain.

"All right, fine," Denali said. "Don't get grumpy. Is your friend Raahi here too?"

"Yes, at camp." Kanvar motioned for Denali to take Frost and Miki and go. He feared the meeting between LaShawn and Karishi, between father and son, would be even more tense than the meeting between Karishi and his grandfather.

"Don't worry, I've got this handled," Karishi told Kanvar as Denali and his companions disappeared into the trees. Tazeran slithered to the rock-fall on the far side of the pool and up the cliffs above it, poking his head into cracks, and licking and clawing at the rocks. Karishi went to the boat and slid out a metal staff that he'd fashioned to look like ivy grew up around it. It was burnished green and was set with an emerald at the top.

Kanvar sucked in an impressed breath. He'd never seen any of Karishi's handiwork beyond his amazing armor. Karishi tossed the staff to Kanvar and pulled out a large cloth-wrapped bundle. "Is he up in the house then?" he asked Kanvar.

"Yes. He's up there." Kanvar could feel LaShawn stewing in the house, unhappy that so many people had descended into his sanctuary, afraid that they would come and see him.

"Will you excuse us for a few minutes, Grandfather?" Karishi hefted the bundle over his shoulder, lifted another out and tucked it under his arm, and started up the trail. "Come on, Kanvar," he called back. "I'm going to need that staff."

"What's he up to?" Lord Theodoric asked.

Kanvar shrugged, waved to Dharanidhar, and followed Karishi to the house.

Chapter Ten

Karishi stopped in front of the crude wooden door and waited for Kanvar to catch up. *Amar says he's touchy about his condition?* he said to Kanvar.

Kanvar nodded. *Very.*

You go first. Tell him I'm here and that I'm coming in to see him one way or another.

Kanvar put his hand against the door and pressed to open it, but found it barred. "LaShawn," he called. "It's Kanvar. Let me in."

No movement or sound came from inside the house.

Kanvar shrugged. "You'll have to manipulate it open," he said to Karishi.

"My hands are full." Snorting in annoyance, Karishi slammed his shoulder against the door. The wood splintered beneath the weight and power of his body. The bar cracked and the door sprang open. "After you," Karishi told Kanvar.

Kanvar stepped into the house and found LaShawn frowning beside the table. "Go away, Kanvar. You promised you wouldn't disturb me."

"True. But you don't think *I* just beat your door down, do you? I'm not nearly strong enough for that."

LaShawn shuffled back behind the low table. It almost hid the stumps of his legs, but his half-stature could not be overlooked. "Who?"

"Your son, Karishi."

LaShawn sucked in a panicked breath and shook his head.

"Don't worry." Kanvar leaned the staff against the wall. "It will be over soon enough. Just meet him, and it will be done with. Come on in, Karishi."

The door swung open all the way, and Karishi strode in. He took one look around the room, went to the straw-stuffed mattress on the floor, and set his bundles down beside it. "Greetings, Father." Karishi spoke while untying the strings that held the smaller of the two bundles. He kept his eyes on what he was doing and didn't look at LaShawn. "I've made you something King Amar thought you might want." He got the strings loose and flipped back an edge of the fabric. Tucked in the fabric, lay a pair of perfectly formed metal legs, feet and all, the color of sun-bronzed skin. "The ankles are spring jointed," Karishi said.

"The legs will seem awkward at first, but after a while you'll walk like any other man. Come here; I'll help you put them on."

"You made those?" LaShawn's voice was husky with awe.

"I make a lot of things. I'll fashion some for your dragon next, but that will take a bit more time." He motioned for LaShawn to sit on the bed and busied himself unbuckling a web of soft leather straps while LaShawn edged over and sat down. "You can wear the harness above or beneath your clothes, whichever is most comfortable," Karishi said as he looped a belt around LaShawn's waist and straightened front and back straps down toward LaShawn's knees. Cross pieces wrapped around his upper and lower thigh to hold the straps in place. Karishi lifted the first leg, set the padded top-side against the stump of LaShawn's right knee, and buckled it into the harness. A final thick padded strap just above the knee cinched the leg tight into place.

Wonder, hope, and fear played across LaShawn's face as Karishi attached the second leg as he had the first. Karishi stepped back and rubbed his chin, examining his work. He adjusted a couple of the straps, then tightened everything down and held out a hand to LaShawn. "I think it will work. Stand up."

LaShawn grabbed his hand, and Karishi pulled him to his feet, keeping his right hand in LaShawn's to steady him.

"Kanvar, the staff." Karishi held out his left hand, and Kanvar set the staff in it. "Here." Karishi passed the staff to LaShawn.

LaShawn took it and used it to steady himself on his new legs. He shook his head in amazement. "Karishi, I . . . I don't know what to say."

"Greetings, Son. I'm glad to meet you, might work for a start."

Smiling, Kanvar let himself out of the house and limped back down to where Dharanidhar was polishing off a draught of his medicine.

That went well, Dharanidhar rumbled.

"Yes, it did." Kanvar sat down beside the pool and tossed pebbles into the water. "Father didn't tell me he had that planned."

Well, he wanted it to be a surprise. There are other things you don't know yet as well, Things King Amar and General Chandran decided after Kumar Raza left. We need to hold a war council: you, I, Lord Theodoric, and Kumar Raza. LaShawn, Karishi, Raahi, and Denali too if they wish. There is much that needs to be done. Though your inability to get the singing stones has overthrown much of their plans, and contingencies will have to be made. Dharanidhar set aside the barrel that held his medicine and licked his lips. *That's the last I have brewed, but I bought more herbs there in the boat. They will last me a while. And I think I'm getting stronger. The more I fly, a little at a time so I don't strain myself, the better my wing feels, and my legs.*

"Good," Kanvar said, delighted to hear that Dharanidhar's health was improving. "Kumar Raza should be back this evening. We'll have to wait to have our war council until then."

Fine by me. I can wait. Dharanidhar shook his head. *Wake up Kivi, it's time to go hunting. Time to find food.*

Kivi hissed in excitement. Dharanidhar chuckled and launched himself in the air. A few minutes later, Karishi and LaShawn came walking down to the pool. LaShawn wore a set of silver armor burnished a pale green to match the staff he used to help him walk. With the armor over the harness and metal legs, LaShawn looked as perfect as any other man. Only a slight stiffness in his gait hinted at his condition.

Kanvar grinned. "That is the most beautiful sight I've ever seen."

As the caravan plodded across the grasslands, a dark form took shape on the horizon—a mountain, far away, bathed in glorious mist. Stonefountain. Aadi watched it with anticipation. The caravan would reach it within a few days. A thundercloud hung over the great mountain, and lightning bolts dazzled the sky with their power. The image of the beautiful city that Lord Taral had lit in Aadi's heart burned through him, and he urged Jenna to run faster in their duties.

Jenna purred between his knees, sensing his determination and joy. Aadi rubbed her sleek scales as she loped back from delivering a requisition of blue cloth for the tailor jati from the weavers. A vast herd of trihorns grazed in the grass, ignoring the caravan with its lowing bovinders, thundering wagons, and chattering humans. Storm clouds hung low over the sky, heavy with rain. A stiff wind bent the grass and sent Aadi's hair slapping his face as he raced along. Thunder rumbled.

"Come on, Jenna," Aadi said. "We've got to find Eashan and get our next task."

A sheet of lightning played across the sky, and Jenna turned skittish.

Easy there, Jenna. Aadi sent reassuring thoughts into her mind. Jenna calmed, thank the fountain, just before Eashan stepped out from behind the scribe wagon and saw him. He handed a scroll up to Aadi.

"A requisition for food supplies for dinner. Get it to the farmer jati quickly unless you want to go hungry tonight," Eashan said.

"Yes, sir." Aadi turned Jenna around and headed back the way he'd come. Thunder rumbled again, and a light spray of rain slapped his face. He shivered, though the rain wasn't cold and there wasn't much moisture at all compared to the storms in Kundiland. Jenna was nervous. She did not like the thunder.

"It's just a little thunderstorm, Jenna," Aadi said. "You have heard thunder before. Relax."

Jenna grumbled and dropped into a stubborn walk. Aadi tried to decide if he should force her to move faster, taking command like the keeper had told him he must, or if he should give Jenna a break for a bit. They had been working hard all day.

"Mama?" A troubled cry reached his ears.

He turned Jenna toward the sound and saw a small girl had fallen behind from whatever Jati she was supposed to be with. She stumbled away from the caravan. The sheet lightning illuminated her tear-streaked face.

"Mama. Mama." The girl's shrill cries twisted Aadi's heart. He hesitated, knowing how important it was that he keep to his duties. Surely, someone was already looking for the child and would find her shortly.

A shadow passed by overhead. Aadi looked up to see Lord Fistas and his dragon. They flew by once and then came back around. Aadi swore. The girl was too far from the wagons. Aadi had no idea what Fistas would do if he caught her. Aadi jumped down from Jenna's back, and leading Jenna behind him, raced out after the child. He could not ride Jenna out there; she might accidentally trample the little girl. Aadi had almost reached the child when he heard the crunch of Fistas's dragon landing behind him.

"Stop." Lord Fistas's command froze Aadi where he stood. Cracking his whip, Lord Fistas came up beside Aadi. Jenna startled back in fear, but the reins clutched in Aadi's frozen hands, kept her in check.

"Mama," the child screamed then broke into wracking sobs.

"Stop crying," Lord Fistas ordered.

The girl gasped and fell silent.

"She's lost," Aadi said. "You can't blame her for crying. I'm going to take her to her parents."

"That is not your job," Lord Fistas snapped. "It's mine, and I warned you once before about leaving the caravan. I don't give second chances."

Aadi sent his mind out searching for Lord Taral, hoping against hope he would be close by, but Aadi could not sense him. "My Lord," Aadi said, trying to staunch the wave of fear that threatened to drown him. "I understand you have to punish me, but let me take the child to her parents first." If he could keep the little girl from being hurt, he would have at least accomplished something.

Lord Fistas sneered. "So, you would take this girl and find her parents instead of delivering the food requisition for dinner?"

Aadi's hand went to the scroll he had tucked into the leather pouch he used to carry his writing supplies and the requisition orders. "The life of a child is worth a late dinner."

Lord Fistas snorted. "A Naga child, not this human filth."

Aadi plucked up more courage than he thought possible. "Do you want to rebuild Stonefountain with your own hands? If you do, go ahead, kill the child, whip me to death, kill us all. You and the other Naga Lords can reconstruct the buildings, plant the farmlands, cook and clean and weave and forge all by yourselves. You don't need humans for anything, except for every dirty job you don't want to perform."

Lord Fistas flushed and his eyes hardened. A forked bolt of lightning flashed on the horizon, followed by two more, each closer than the last. A shock of thunder rattled the wagons. "I'm going to kill you, boy. I'll whip every last strip of flesh from your bones and stake you out to let lizards and ants feast on what's left."

Lightning struck again, and thunder sounded, rolling and swelling until it shook the ground. Lord Fistas looked away from Aadi and gasped. The thousands of trihorns that had been grazing peacefully moments before had been startled by the lightning and were stampeding toward the caravan. The lead ones passed Aadi on both sides.

Lord Fistas swore and raced to his dragon. "Fly, fly!"

As the Naga Lord and his dragon lifted off, Aadi gained control of himself. Jenna screamed and reared in terror at the wall of thundering trihorns that bore down on them. Her thrashing front claws tore through Aadi's arm and shoulder. He screamed in pain and released her.

Jenna bolted.

The little girl, still unable to cry, stretched her arms out to Aadi, pleading with her eyes for him to help her. He snatched her up and raced back toward the wagons, but realized in a heartbeat he would never make it. The trihorns were already upon him, great lumbering monsters. The ones that had already passed him, smashed into the wagons, splintering the wood, and trampling overtop of them as if they were no more than mounds of dirt, with the rest of the herd following in an unchecked wave of destruction. Everyone in the caravan would be trampled. Thousands of people would die.

Aadi turned to face the thundering herd. A flash of lightning to his left almost blinded him with its power. Trumpeting in fear, the stampeding trihorns turned a fraction to the right, the main bulk of them still heading for the caravan.

Aadi blinked the light from his eyes. The trihorns were terrified of the lightning.

He gasped, fighting the panic that rooted him to the spot only feet from the wall of speeding flesh, he focused his mind, imagined a great bolt of lightning striking where he stood, and projected it into the minds of the trihorns.

The shoulder of a trihorn knocked him to the ground as it swerved suddenly away from him.

He rolled to his knees, still clutching the little girl and imagined lightning striking him again and again and again, blasting the image into the minds of the trihorns.

The trihorns turned.

Aadi imagined a wall of forked lightning striking down the length of the caravan. In a roll of thunder and shaking ground, the trihorns wheeled around and raced away from the caravan.

Aadi gasped for breath as the herd retreated. A dizzying emptiness swept over him. The pain of his slashed arm and shoulder felt like nothing in the face of the utter agony that consumed him. Something was gone, something missing. Half of himself had been torn away. Perhaps he had been struck by lightning.

"Cristyann, my baby." A woman rushed out from the caravan and lifted the little girl from Aadi's arms.

Aadi remained on his knees, unable to move, searching for the part of himself that had gone missing. He saw a crumpled lump of flesh off in the trampled grass, tan scales with black lightning-shaped stripes.

"Jenna!" Aadi struggled to his feet and raced over to the fallen camdor. Her neck was broken and her head lay twisted at an odd angle. Her legs were splayed out beside her, her body crushed by the trihorns. Aadi put a hand on her flank. Her skin, though still warm, was lifeless. And he knew he was dead with her. The utter despair, which Jenna had kept at bay, devoured Aadi's heart.

He screamed and kept screaming until Lord Fistas grabbed his shoulder.

"Silence, boy."

His final scream stuck in his throat, and he shuddered, lowering his head and squeezing his eyes closed.

"What's wrong with him? Is he hurt?" Lord Taral's voice seemed to come from far away.

"His arm and shoulder, but I don't think that's why he was screaming," Lord Fistas answered. "It's his mind, Taral. It feels like the dragon sickness. He's far gone in it."

A hand pressed against Aadi's forehead. "He doesn't have a fever." Lord Fistas tore the front of Aadi's shirt open. "No rash. I don't understand it."

Sweat drenched Aadi like rain. He started shaking and couldn't stop.

"Aadi." Lord Taral touched his injured shoulder, and he shrank away.

"It's all right. Hold still." Taral eased Aadi's shirt off him and slathered Great dragon saliva over his wounds.

"It's no use," Aadi whimpered. "She's gone. You can't save her."

"Aadi, you're not bound to that camdor," Lord Taral said. "You won't die just because she has."

"No. Jenna." Aadi wrapped his arms around Jenna's neck and buried his face against her flesh.

"We have to take him to the king," Lord Fistas said.

"We can't both leave the caravan. Not after what's just happened." Lord Taral slipped into Aadi's mind and got hold of his body, easing him away from the fallen camdor. "You should take him, Fistas. I'll see to the care of the humans here."

Lord Fistas cleared his throat. "Whichever of us brings him to the king is likely to gain His Majesty's notice and favor. I know how much that means to you, Taral. You've long sought to serve in the Elite Guard. I don't really care about that. So, you take him."

"Fistas, these people are frightened and need help, not your . . . less than gentle ways."

Lord Fistas jerked Aadi to his feet and shoved him toward Taral's dragon. "Don't worry, I'll be gentle. I'm just as capable of calming frightened humans as I am of scaring them. You go. Take the boy. He's going to be a very powerful Naga if he can already turn stampeding trihorns. By the fountain, I would never have thought to do it that way. In fact, I was at a loss of what to do at all."

Lord Taral got an arm under Aadi's shoulders and helped him onto the gold dragon's back. Taral eased in place behind Aadi, and the dragon took flight. Aadi kept his eyes closed and his arms wrapped around himself, too overcome with the emptiness inside to do anything else. Lord Taral kept him upright with a strong arm around his waist.

"Aadi, you've had Naga training already?" Taral's soft voice questioned. "You must have, to control your mind well enough to keep the dragon sickness hidden from me and stop those trihorns. Who trained you?"

Aadi shook his head and refused to answer. He rebuilt the shields around his mind, strong and tight, wishing he could shield himself from the memories of happy days in the palace, sporting with the young gold dragons, his tedious studies with Parmver, his quiet talks with King Amar, and pleasant afternoons with Devaj teaching him how to wield a sword. But all of that was gone, utterly destroyed.

"You're from Kundiland, you said. Did you know the king? Have you met King Amar? I wish I could have before he died. It would have been such an honor."

Aadi moaned.

"He's dead. I know," Lord Taral said, his voice filled with regret. "We flew so hard to get here in time to save him, and we failed. At least his son sits on the throne. Thank the fountain King Khalid has left the realm of the dead and returned to help him. His Majesty Devaj's task and burden are far too great for one so young to face alone."

At the mention of Khalid's name, Aadi struggled to speak through his despair. "Khalid is evil, My Lord. I swear to you, he is. You don't know the things I know, what I've seen, what I've been through. King Amar has forbidden me to go to him. Please, I have to get to Stonefountain, to the Great Gold dragons to bond. There is one named Jaymon, a son of the royal guard. We've grown up together and long planned—" Aadi choked and could not speak again for a few moments. Breathing seemed an impossible chore.

"King Amar told you to stay away from His Majesty, Khalid? How could he? King Amar died before His Majesty Devaj raised Khalid from the fountain. You are hurt and confused. The dragon sickness has your mind all twisted up. Only the king can help you. Only he can select the gold dragons for you to choose from. Don't worry, Aadi, His Majesty will get you through this. You'll be all right in no time, and I'll visit you and Jaymon in the palace and brag to everyone how you saved an entire caravan of humans."

Aadi's shaking lessened, and his breathing became a little easier. Whenever Lord Taral talked to him, the world made sense. The brightness of Taral's voice and the faith with which he spoke drove away the darkness inside.

"Good boy," Lord Taral said. "Everything is going to be all right. I promise you."

Chapter Eleven

Rain had started falling in earnest by the time Lord Taral's dragon neared the mountain. It pounded the Maran and Varnan soldiers who worked like ants on the slopes of the mountain and the city below, rebuilding the fallen mansions, redigging the sewer systems, and repaving the streets. It slicked the scales of the blue dragons, chained and forced to lift the heaviest stones into place.

The greatest work was being done on the palace itself. Its sweeping halls and magnificent chambers had already taken shape. Here, the Great Gold dragons of the Kundiland pride worked tirelessly alongside the humans to construct an edifice worthy of their king. Aadi recognized some of them, but they were all the older dragons he'd never spent time with. He saw no sign of the younger dragons of the pride. Desperate, he sent his thoughts out looking for Jaymon, but he could not find him.

"Don't worry. His Majesty will find your friend." Lord Taral's reassurance washed over Aadi as it had through the whole flight. It was Lord Taral's strength that had kept him calm and breathing.

Saanjh, Lord Taral's dragon, flared his wings and swooped into the palace. Thunder and lightning continued outside along with the rain as Taral helped Aadi down from the dragon and walked him into an adjoining chamber where several Nagas were gathered around a desk coordinating the reconstruction. The oldest of them looked up with a sheaf of papers in his hands and a harried look in his eyes.

Lord Taral bowed to him. "Greetings, Lord Jesson."

"Taral, what are you doing here?" Jesson snapped. "How fares the caravan?"

"Wretchedly," Taral said, keeping a steadying hand on Aadi. "The lightning spooked a herd of trihorns, stampeding them into the caravan. We came close to losing every last wagon and human."

Aadi shivered.

"Close? How many are lost?" The harried look faded from Lord Jesson's eyes replaced by serious concern.

"Only two wagons and one camdor because of this boy." Lord Taral squeezed Aadi's shoulder.

"How could one boy save the caravan from a stampede?" Lord Jesson set the papers down and came over to get a closer look at Aadi.

"He's a Naga, sir. Not bonded yet, but well trained . . . in King Amar's court I'm guessing. He used his power to turn the trihorns away. It was the most amazing thing I've ever seen. I would have waited to bring him here until the whole caravan came in, but he's deep in the dragon sickness. Feels close to death to me. He needs immediate attention from the king."

"Yes, I guess he does," Lord Jesson said. "And I suppose the caravan is in total disarray."

"Fistas is taking care of it."

"Ha. Right. Get back there now before he does more damage than the trihorns."

"Yes, My Lord." Lord Taral released Aadi and turned to go.

The moment Taral's mind left Aadi's, it felt like he'd plunged into a suffocating black lake. He gasped. Taral turned back, but Lord Jesson waved him away. "The king can do more for him than you can. Return to your work."

Lord Taral nodded and strode away.

Lord Jesson got hold of Aadi. "You're soaked and half naked. You can't go to the king like this." He turned to the other men in the room. "Unenong, go see if the king is available. Phyric, find him some dry clothes and get him cleaned up."

"Yes, sir." Phyric motioned for Aadi to follow him.

Aadi wavered, but remained rooted in place. It took so much effort just to breathe, and his mind was so empty. Somewhere in the deepest reaches of his thoughts he reminded himself he was supposed to stay away from

Khalid. He must run now, escape and hide, but his body refused to move.

"Come on," Lord Phyric said, grabbing Aadi's arm.

Aadi cried out at the sudden pressure and wrench on his healing camdor wound. The skin had closed over, but his arm still ached.

"What—" Phyric released him and examined the livid scars across his shoulder and arm. "—happened?"

Aadi shuddered. "My camdor . . . she spooked. Died. I'm going to die."

"You're not going to die." Lord Phyric grabbed his other arm and propelled him out of the room, down a wide hall, and into another chamber where supply chests were stacked in orderly rows. He opened one, and got out a towel. From another he pulled a silk shirt, trousers, and a warm vest. *"Dry yourself and put these on."* He shoved them into Aadi's arms and left him there to change.

Aadi might have just stood there staring at the wall if Lord Phyric's last words hadn't been a powerful command that forced Aadi to obey. When Aadi had dressed, he stepped out of the supply room thinking this might be his best chance to escape, but he found Lord Jesson waiting outside.

"Come with me," Jesson ordered.

In his weakened state, Aadi had no hope of fighting his command. He followed Lord Jesson toward the center of the palace. It was laid out much like the palace in Kundiland, except it was larger in every aspect. Wider halls, gigantic chambers, vaulted ceilings, and more rooms than Aadi wanted to count. The stone on the lower parts of the walls looked weathered and ancient, while higher up, the stone had been newly cut and set in place. As of yet, there was no gold leafing, leaving the stone naked to the eye.

Lord Jesson urged Aadi up a wide stair leading to an expansive double door, which unlike everything else, had been overlaid in gold and etched with the image of Stone-fountain. A pair of Naga Guardsmen flanked the doors, but nodded to Lord Jesson and swung the doors open as he approached.

Lord Jesson guided Aadi inside where gilded walls, floor, ceiling, and pillars sparkled in the light of a giant crystal chandelier that hung from the ceiling. A golden throne was set on a dais at the head of the room. In it sat Devaj, robed in shimmering gold, an intricate golden crown studded with diamonds on his head. His eyes glowed a pale gold, sending a shiver down Aadi's spine.

Devaj rose, and all the Nagas and humans in the hall went to one knee.

Lord Jesson forced Aadi down beside him.

"Aadi, what a surprise." It was Devaj's warm voice that rang out across the hall, startling Aadi. He'd expected King Khalid to sound different, more like the angry rush of evil Aadi had felt in Rajahansa's mind.

Devaj walked down the dais steps and across the vast hall to stand in front of Aadi. "I thought I left you safely at the new village in Kundiland."

Aadi swallowed, battling his fear, emptiness, and pain to speak. Lord Taral was no longer here to give him strength. Aadi called up the very last of his own. "You ordered the villagers to be slaughtered. I don't call that safe. You knew I had the dragon sickness, yet you took all the gold dragons away where I could not reach them. You left me to die. You promised me power and glory and a place at your side, and then you discarded me, just like you did to—"

Aadi had meant to say Rajahansa, but Khalid's mind wrapped around Aadi's own, blocking him so he could not utter a sound.

"Yes, of course, I promised you a place here with me." Devaj's voice was still warm, in stark contrast to the fierce coldness of Khalid's mind. "And you will have it as soon as you've bonded. You've been like a little brother to me for so long." He put a gentle hand on Aadi's shoulder. "Who told you I ordered the villagers slaughtered? I would never do such a thing. In fact, I left five of my best men in Kundiland to make sure they would be safe. Captain Vitra, the commander of my Elite Naga Guard was there. It's strange though, I've heard nothing from him for a long time now. Did you see him before you left Kundiland? How did you come to be here in Varna?"

Khalid released Aadi's voice so he could speak, but kept a firm hold on his mind.

"Your Majesty, I-I don't know." Cold terror speared Aadi, and he threw a shield up around the parts of his mind that knew anything about the happenings in Kundiland. General Chandran had accused him of intending to betray King Amar and all his plans to Khalid. That had never been Aadi's intent, but he realized there were things he knew that Amar probably didn't want Khalid to find out. The fact that King Amar was alive, for one. Was there more? Aadi had no idea what knowledge he might have that Khalid would be able to use against Aadi's king and friends.

"Come now, you must know something." Devaj rubbed a hand across Aadi's forehead while Khalid's mind like a sickening trickle of filth caressed his shields. "Just tell me what happened. How did you get here?"

Aadi shuddered at the feel of Khalid's mind in his own. "I took a boat from the village. I'm looking for Jaymon."

Devaj chuckled. "You paddled across the ocean in a dugout canoe? That doesn't seem likely."

"Please, can I see Jaymon?"

Devaj dropped his hand from Aadi's head and eased the pressure away from Aadi's shields. "You think you're ready to bond? You don't have a fever."

"I-I know, but I'm dying. I'm so alone. Something happened because of the ointment Rajahansa and Haidar used on me. I need to bond. Please, grant me a Choosing Ceremony." Hope blossomed in Aadi. Maybe, just maybe, there was enough of Devaj left that he would be able to convince Khalid not to harm him and to allow him to bond. Why else would Khalid have pulled back from stripping all the information he wanted from Aadi's mind? Aadi had no illusion that his pitiful shields could have stopped Khalid.

"Of course, my little friend. A Choosing Ceremony you shall have. One every day until you come down with the fever. And the moment the fever starts, we'll have the grandest of all Bonding Ceremonies, and I will make you steward of the palace." Devaj grinned and his golden eyes sparkled.

Aadi gasped. Lord Taral had been right. King Khalid was not evil at all. Everything bad that had happened at the Kundiland palace must have been Rajahansa's, Haidar's, and Liander's doing. "Thank you, thank you." Aadi took Devaj's hand and kissed the back of it.

Devaj lifted Aadi's chin with a gentle hand. *I will grant you everything I just promised on one condition; you answer my questions. What has happened in Kundiland, and how did you get here?* he spoke into Aadi's mind so no one else in the hall could hear him.

Before Aadi could respond, Khalid rushed back into his mind. No longer a trickle, the force of Khalid's power was a torrent of foul blackness that washed aside Aadi's shields and consumed everything, absorbing every detail and memory of Aadi's life since Devaj had left him at the new village. *So, King Amar is alive,* Khalid mused. *I wonder how that filthy halfblood, General Chandran, and Rajan defeated my Nagas at the Maran Colony. It's too bad you don't know.* Khalid sent daggers of fiery pain raking through Aadi's mind as if that could jar loose a memory Aadi did not have. He had not been present when King Amar and the others made their plans or when the colony was attacked, and he'd left before everyone else returned. He knew only that King Amar had been victorious.

Aadi screamed in pain, but Khalid kept any sound from passing through Aadi's lips.

No, you don't know anything useful, only that General Chandran and the dragon hunters have gone to Varna and Maran, no doubt to lead some kind of insurrection against me. Stupid fool, boy. Khalid released Aadi's mind.

Devaj walked away from Aadi, returning to his throne. "I'm glad you're here, Aadi. Until you come down with the fever, you may be my personal servant so we can spend plenty of time together." His eyes twinkled and the congenial smile on his face was heartwarming. "Do you remember the time we snuck down into Parmver's lab and sampled his mushrooms?" Devaj laughed. "Oh, Aadi, it brightens my day just seeing you. Lord Jesson, take him to my chambers, please. As soon as I'm done here, I'll go in search of some dragons for him."

"Yes, Your Majesty." Lord Jesson tugged Aadi to his feet and guided him out of the throne room. "I had no idea you were such a close friend of the king's," Jesson said as he walked Aadi down a long hall and into a set of rooms which had been restored, complete with lush carpets, tapestries, and furniture.

Aadi gritted his teeth and said nothing. The face Khalid put on for the world and the cruelty of his mind were in such opposition to each other it left Aadi breathless.

"Here you are," Lord Jesson said, surveying the room. "Since you are to serve him, I suggest you make yourself useful and tidy up in here. Looks like no one's been in yet to do that today."

"Yes, My Lord." Aadi stumbled over to a discarded night robe and lifted it from the floor. "I'll have it clean in no time." Serving a king was something Aadi knew well. He'd been doing it for King Amar for quite some time, trading off the work with others of the young dragons.

He forced through the emptiness in his heart to make his body work. At least it didn't take much thought to straighten bed covers and dust wall hangings. He kept his mind focused on the bright hope Devaj had offered him. He would have a Choosing Ceremony. He'd get to be around the gold dragons, and surely that would trigger his fever. By tomorrow he could be bonded and serving as steward instead of chamber boy. It was enough hope to keep him breathing and working, to keep him alive for now.

A couple of hours later, Aadi had put the king's chambers in perfect order, sweeping, organizing, and polishing until the room gleamed. He had just finished brushing the last bit of dust from the windowsill when Devaj strode into the room. Aadi stiffened until he saw Devaj carried a golden robe over his arm.

"Your Majesty." Aadi went to one knee.

"Well, Aadi. Here's your robe. I'm quite excited for your Choosing Ceremony. It's going to be . . . entertaining. Here, put this on." Devaj drew Aadi to his feet and draped the robe over Aadi's shoulders. An elaborate representation of Stonefountain had been embroidered into it.

"It's amazing," Aadi said, running his hands down the shimmering fabric.

Devaj smiled. "I have a present for you. It's a very special gift that I only give to very special people." He pressed an oblong silver box into Aadi's hands. The box was fashioned so the hinge and catch were dragons twining about it.

"It's beautiful," Aadi said. He undid the catch and lifted the lid back. Resting inside on black velvet was a silver dagger. Like the dragons twined around the box, a silver dragon wrapped around the hilt. The pommel was a heart clutched in the dragon's claws.

Aadi sucked in a breath and reached for the hilt. As he touched it, a whisper of indecipherable voices brushed his mind. Aadi drew his hand back. "What was that?"

"Those are friends, Aadi. This is a very special dagger. As long as you have it, you will never be alone. And some day, when you're ready, you will join them."

Devaj's voice was as warm as ever, but Aadi sensed a cold twist of menace from Khalid. Aadi closed the box with a gentle click. "Thank you. I am unworthy of such a gift."

Devaj chuckled. "Yet I have given it to you anyway. It pleases me to see it in your hands. Now come. The dragons are waiting for you."

Aadi slipped the box into a pocket of his robe and followed Devaj out of the hall and back to the throne room. It had been cleared of people other than Aadi and Devaj, but five Great Gold dragons waited, gathered in a semi-circle around the sunburst carved into the golden floor. They were all older dragons that Aadi did not recognize.

Aadi hesitated as Devaj lead him up to them. "Where's Jaymon?"

Devaj's voice took on a stern edge. "It is the king's decision which dragons are suitable for you to choose from. Jaymon is too young and weak. He passed none of my tests. Try the minds of these five. If you find none that call to you, I will bring five more tomorrow, and the day after, and the day after, as long as it takes for you to find the dragon that will be your most suitable companion."

"Your Majesty, can Jaymon try the tests again. I know he was well trained in everything at the palace in Kundiland. I'm sure he will not fail a second time." Aadi felt uncomfortable by the size and unfamiliarity of the gathered dragons. Their eyes seemed cold to him.

"Of course he can try again," Devaj said. "As many times as he likes until you come down with the fever and choose someone else."

"I don't think I can choose anyone else," Aadi said.

Devaj grabbed his arm in an icy grip. "Don't be stubborn. Go to these dragons and test their minds." He thrust Aadi out into the center of the dragons.

Frightened and breathing hard, Aadi turned to face each one. The first one on the left bowed, lowering his head so Aadi could touch its dragonstone. Aadi stepped over to it, reached out his hand, and rested it on the dragonstone. A shock like icy water doused his mind, so cold it burned. Aadi snatched his hand back gasping.

The dragon growled, ruffled its wings, and stepped back. The next one in the circle bowed and lowered its head. Shaking, Aadi reached out his hand once more. As his fingers touched the stone, his mind felt like it was enveloped in molten gold. Silky and thick, it pulled him under and kept him there. He searched for the dragon's mind and memories. This touch was supposed to be a chance for the two of them to see into the deepest reaches of each other's soul to determine if they were right for each other. But Aadi sensed no thoughts, saw no images. He was submerged alone in a pool of golden magma. It pressed in around him, filling his mouth and lungs, suffocating him. He thrashed to get away, but found no surface to reach, no shore to swim to.

Help me, he screamed.

Devaj grabbed him and pulled him away from the dragon, freeing Aadi from its mind. "Well, that one isn't it," Devaj said with a chuckle.

The second dragon retreated, and the third one bowed. Aadi stood frozen in place. He dared not touch another one.

"Would you rather die?" Devaj asked him.

Aadi shook his head. He didn't want to die. He could only hope being around the dragons would bring on his fever, and he would find one he was compatible with.

"Try the next one," Devaj said.

Aadi licked his lips and shuffled forward.

Greetings little one, the dragon said as Aadi neared. Aadi did not hear the words clearly. As usual he had to content himself with feeling the meaning behind them. He reached out and put his hand on the golden stone. He felt the dragon's mind faint and far away, but when he tried to move toward it, it slipped even further from him. He tried harder to reach it, but the essence of the dragon was always just beyond his mind.

I feel nothing, the dragon said. He pulled away from Aadi and stepped back. The emptiness Aadi had felt when

Jenna died ripped through him once more. He cried out and dropped to his knees.

Devaj wrenched him to his feet and shook him. "You're not trying, Aadi. I expect you to at least try." He forced Aadi over to the next dragon and slapped Aadi's hand down on its dragonstone. The stone burned through Aadi's hand, up his arm, and across his mind—searing fire and pain. He thrashed to get away, but Devaj held him in place. *Take a good look,* Khalid said into his mind. *See what it is to be a Naga.*

Aadi tried to look into the dragon's mind, but all he felt was fire and pain. When at last Devaj released him and he stumbled back, he was drenched in sweat and shaking so hard his teeth chattered.

The dragon stepped away and the final dragon bowed. "Go." Devaj pushed Aadi toward it.

"No, please. I can't." Aadi dared not face any more torment.

The dragon let out a gentle rumble, eased forward and rubbed his head along Aadi's chest and side. A terrible longing washed over Aadi. He wanted this dragon, needed a bond with it. "Please," Aadi whispered. "Please don't hurt me."

Why would I hurt you, the dragon said. *It is a great honor to be chosen to bond with a Naga. Let me see your soul, little one, and I will show you mine.*

Reassured, Aadi placed his hand on the dragon's stone. Aadi's mind dropped into a pit full of bloodlusted raptors. They tore into him, claw and teeth, tearing great gouges from his soul and devouring him in a frenzy. He fell before them into unconsciousness.

When he woke, he found himself prostrate on the golden sunburst, drenched with sweat, too weak to move. His mind was empty save for a searing loneliness. The room was empty except for Devaj who leaned over him and felt his forehead.

"Hm. Still no fever. Well, I suppose we'll have to try again tomorrow."

Aadi moaned.

"Get up," Devaj ordered, his voice held none of its warmth, only Khalid's coldness. "Fetch my dinner to my chambers. I'll eat alone tonight. It's been a grueling day."

Aadi tried to get up, but his body refused to move.

"Come now. You can't be so weak already. That would spoil all my fun." *Get up!* Khalid ordered. His command ripped through Aadi's mind and snapped him to his feet. *Fetch my dinner, boy. It had better be in my room by the time I get there.*

Aadi stumbled away in search of the palace kitchens.

Chapter Twelve

Days passed, each one a greater torment than the last. Every time Aadi touched the dragons Khalid had brought for him, he felt the most exquisite pain. He thought he was dying over and over again, but each time he awoke still alive, sick and weak, Khalid's taunts ringing in his mind. *Come on, Aadi. You're a Naga. You can feel the dragons. You could link with them, but you're not trying. Try harder, Aadi. Trust. Give yourself over to them. Here's the chalice, Aadi. Hold it. Feel it. It will be filled with blood the moment you come down with the fever.*

And still the fever never touched him. He lost track of days and hours serving Khalid, given the most menial of chores: polishing Khalid's armor, scrubbing the garbage chutes, washing Khalid's clothes and bedding. Aadi could no longer think of him as Devaj, though Khalid looked like Devaj on the outside, though he fooled all the other Nagas around him, Aadi could sense only Khalid's cold cruelty.

Dragonbound VIII

At night, Aadi stayed in a small bedchamber just off Khalid's room. He lay awake, staring into the darkness, imagining he heard the whisper of voices. They swirled around his mind, but he could never make out what they were saying. One night, lost in the abyss of his torment, Aadi remembered the gift Khalid had given him that first day. He crawled over to the dirty, sweat-streaked robe, which he wore each day when he went to see the dragons, and pulled out the silver box. It glowed faintly in the blackness. And the voices whispered to him. *Open the clasp. Open the box. Draw us out.*

Aadi caressed the dragon on the box then flicked the lid open. The little dagger lay inside, the pommel heart pulsing with a silver light. He touched the handle and the voices swirled inside him, sweeping through the vast emptiness, becoming a part of him. But instead of relieving his loneliness, they increased it, as if they too were lonely, empty vessels in search of their missing souls. *Join us, they cried. Come into the darkness.*

Revolted, Aadi told himself to let go of the dagger and close the lid, but his hand pulled it from the box instead. If he had to be alone, wasn't it better to be lonely in their company. He lay back on the bed and pressed the flat of the dagger against his chest. The ghostly voices flitted in and out of him, sharing his despair.

From that night on, Aadi wore the dagger tucked inside his vest. He no longer saw the world around him in its color and beauty. His eyes only saw shades of gray and black. When people spoke to him, their voices were far away. The food he ate had no flavor. Everything was muted, except for his daily torment with the dragons. Each new day, Khalid made him touch the stones of five more dragons. Always strangers to him. Never Jaymon or the other young dragons from the Kundiland palace. With each new dragon waited another torture more wicked than the last. Day-by-day, Aadi grew weaker, until it took him an hour just to make Khalid's bed and two hours to sew on a button. And Khalid reveled in every moment of his agony, taunting him—*You're a Naga, Aadi. What's wrong with you? Why can't you bond? Why have you no fever?*

Indumauli pushed upriver in the clear black water, grateful to have at last found the river that would take him to Stonefountain. *I never want to go near the ocean again*, he fumed. *Salt water, what a nightmare.* If he would have known how sick and weak the ocean would make him, how close to death he would come before reaching his goal, he doubted he would have volunteered so quickly to take Aadi to Stonefountain. But that was behind him now. Ahead, lights twinkled on the mountainside and from multitudes of buildings below it. Indumauli lifted his head out of the water to take in the night-shrouded city. Stonefountain was supposed to be an ancient ruin, but it was no longer. Indumauli's heart swelled as he witnessed the grandeur of the past reborn. A shiver rippled along his body. Khalid had done this. Khalid had restored Stonefountain just as Rajahansa had promised he would.

Rajahansa, Rajahansa, Indumauli murmured, *did you see this vision before it became reality? Was it so wrong for you to side with Khalid?*

Indumauli's head swayed back and forth with the gentle lapping of the water. Stonefountain was restored. A Great Gold Dragon King perched once more on his throne, with everyone bowing in homage. It seemed to Indumauli that this was how the world should be, and he wondered why His Majesty Amar had fought so hard against its achievement. Still, thoughts nagged at Indumauli, and the dazzling city lights couldn't quite make him forget how Amar had been chained, Tana and Mani abused, and Parmver murdered. Could not the Great Gold Dragon King be brought back to power without treachery?

Indumauli bared his teeth and hissed. Yes, there had been treachery and betrayal. Rajahansa was not perched on his throne at Stonefountain as Khalid had promised. But was that Khalid's fault, or was that Kanvar's and Tana's fault? They had arranged for Rajahansa's murder. Indumauli shook his head. They'd done it at King Amar's command. Who then was responsible for all the death and suffering? Rajahansa, Khalid, Amar, Kanvar?

Troubled, Indumauli sank back into the water and continued upstream. He kept his mind open, figuring Aadi would be searching for him, but Aadi did not make contact. Indumauli kept low to the bottom of the river as it came alongside human habitation. It was nighttime and the humans should be sleeping, but he couldn't risk being seen. He'd promised Amar he would take care of Aadi, and Indumauli was concerned he and Aadi had been separated for too long. As he swam through the city, he sent out his mind in search of Aadi's as he would if he were looking to speak to another Great dragon. Aadi gave no response, and Indumauli figured he must be sleeping.

Sleep then, little friend, Indumauli said as he neared the waterfall that poured down the face of the mountain from the palace above. *I am going to try and find Rajahansa. I'm confused and can no longer tell who was right between him and Amar.*

Indumauli put on a burst of speed and leaped from the water, spreading his wingfins to carry him up into the waterfall. His flight ended with the roaring water pouring over him as he landed against the stone cliff and started to climb. When he reached the top, he followed the water through a conduit into the heart of the mountain, to Stonefountain itself.

Stonefountain glowed with radiant color emanating from the crystals that grew from the walls. The fountain itself bubbled up in the center of the chamber where the crystals that had once been torn from the walls now rested in the water. Indumauli pulled himself from the river and went to the basin. This was where Devaj had started his association with Khalid's spirit by touching the water. Indumauli plunged his webbed claws into the fountain and called for Rajahansa. He heard no reply.

Hissing, Indumauli pawed through the stones in the water calling out to them. *Talk to me, spirits. I know you are here. Speak. Where is Rajahansa? I must converse with him.*

The chamber remained silent and empty.

Indumauli jerked his claws back from the water and circled the fountain. Tazeran had described the Darvati Hall of Ancestors as alive with song and spirits. Both Kanvar and Devaj had said that the wounded Stonefountain resounded with deafening screams of agony. Indumauli heard nothing. Groaning, he sank to the ground and rested his head on his front claws. *Stupid, Indumauli*, he chided himself. Kanvar and Devaj are Nagas, and only Nagas hear the singing stones. Tazeran hears the song and can converse with the spirits because he's bound to a Naga. Indumauli let out a long sigh. *I am not bound to a Naga and never will be. Rajahansa's spirit is beyond me and will forever remain that way.*

After a minute, he rose to his feet and slid back into the water. Dismally, he climbed back down the cliff, keeping himself buried in the waterfall so no humans would see him. When he reached the base, he found a wide crack in the rock, an inlet where some of the water from the river ran back inside the mountain. The Nagas who had rebuilt the city were aware of the cleft it seemed; an iron grate barred entrance to whatever lay beyond.

Indumauli flicked his wingfins in annoyance and crawled head-first down the grating. It ended deep underwater but left a gap big enough for Indumauli to slip through. Looking for a safe place to make a lair, Indumauli slid under the grate and swam up the narrow channel of dark water. The channel curved and then opened up into a large cavern. Indumauli slid out of the water and shook himself. The scent of molten gold and dragon waste gagged him. He pawed his nose and looked around.

An oil lamp on the far wall lit the chamber with a sickly yellow light, revealing a number of the young Great Gold dragons from the Kundiland pride chained to the rock. The chains were long enough the dragons could reach the water and each other but no farther. The dragons crouched wretchedly trying to avoid their own filth. Their bodies were gaunt and faces starved.

Indumauli, they cried out upon seeing him. *Indumauli, help us.*

Indumauli hissed and went to the closest dragon, Bellori, examining the chains that held him. *Who did this to you?*

Khalid, Bellori said. *We tried to fight him, but we were no match for a Naga.*

Indumauli clawed at the chains and then at the stone where they were anchored, but could tell immediately that it would do no good. *What can I do? How can I help you? I cannot break the chains, and even if I could, there is a grate blocking the exit.*

We have no food, Bellori said. *They do not feed us. If you could bring us some fish, we'd be indebted to you forever.*

Yes, of course, Indumauli said. *Give me a chance to hunt. I'll bring you some.* He crawled into the water and left the wretched young dragons. He'd promised them fish, but wasn't sure he could fulfill that promise. The river had been strangely barren of life, as if it had been polluted for a long time and only just cleansed. Indumauli had barely found enough fish to feed himself, catching enough to feed so many gold dragons seemed impossible. Indumauli's coils rippled in agitation. Khalid. Khalid had chained the children and was starving them to death. No glorious city could justify that. Indumauli should never have doubted King Amar. Khalid was evil. Khalid was the enemy.

Aadi, Indumauli called out. *Aadi, Aadi, where are you? Why haven't you helped your friends?* Still, Indumauli could make no connection with Aadi's mind. He swam back downriver out of the city in search of some place to make his lair. He would keep his promise and feed the young dragons everything he could catch, but he knew it wouldn't be enough to keep them alive.

Wrapped in a world of gray torment, Aadi carried Khalid's empty breakfast tray back to the kitchen. His soul hurt beyond words. He gasped in despair as his legs gave out on him, and he fell to the floor. The golden dishes clattered around him. Fearing the noise would alert someone and bring a reprimand upon him, Aadi crawled away and hid himself behind a tapestry in a room just off the hall.

He pulled the dagger from its hiding place and clasped it against his chest. *We are death*, the voices whispered to him. *Join us. Death is the only escape from the emptiness, the only end to your torment.*

Aadi looked down at the dagger. The blade was long enough one thrust would pierce his heart. That's all it would take, just the willpower for one last move of defiance that would free him from Khalid forever. Gritting his teeth, Aadi twisted the handle out and pressed the tip of the dagger against his left breast.

Footsteps sounded in the hall and a voice he recognized froze his hands.

"Good morning, Lord Jesson." Lord Taral's voice split the gray darkness.

"Taral, it's good to see you. How is the construction coming on the artisan district?" Lord Jesson asked.

Lord Taral chuckled. "Fine, just fine. So well, in fact, it will be finished twice as soon as the work my brother is doing in the manufacturing section."

"That is no surprise to me, Taral. You have a way of inspiring and motivating people that your brother has always lacked."

"That is because Fistas thinks the way to get people to work is through fear and subjugation. He believes that to rule well is to make others serve him. While I, on the other hand, have always maintained the best way to lead is to serve the people who have been entrusted to my care."

With each word Lord Taral spoke, a little color came back into Aadi's sight. He gasped and lowered the dagger.

"I'm not sure I agree with your philosophy, Taral," Lord Jesson said, "but no one can dispute your ability to perform. So, what brings you to the palace?"

"I've come to check on Aadi. I promised him I'd visit and get to know his dragon once he'd bonded. How is he, My Lord? Have you seen him?"

There was silence for a moment and feet shuffling as Lord Jesson drew Lord Taral into the room where Aadi hid. "You haven't heard?" Lord Jesson said in a low voice.

"What?" Lord Taral asked.

Aadi clutched the hilt of the dagger to his chest and squeezed his eyes closed.

"Aadi's a halfblood. He can't bond. He'll never be a Naga. But don't tell him that. The king has been having a good deal of fun with him, dangling the prospect in front of him, letting him go through the Choosing Ceremony again and again. It does nothing but hurt him. He has no fever and never will."

"Are you sure he's a halfblood? He may just be a late bloomer," Lord Taral said.

"Oh, there is no doubt. His Majesty Khalid explained it to me. Kanvar and the other traitors who killed King Amar used an ointment on him that Khalid himself tested and perfected. Spread on a young Naga, the ointment will induce the dragon fever within minutes, an hour at the latest. If used on a human, the human will die immediately as if poisoned by snakelily. But when used on a halfblood, it stirs in them the dragon sickness without the fever. They feel all the sensations a Naga will feel when ready to bond, the emptiness, the dark agony. Only they can't bond, and they won't die, not from the sickness at least. What it does is drive them mad, and eventually they kill themselves."

"But that's cruel," Lord Taral's voice rose.

"Quiet," Lord Jesson warned him. "The king has forbidden anyone to interfere with his little game. The boy is his personal amusement for as long as he lasts. Besides, King Khalid is not as cruel as all that. He gave Aadi a dagger on his first day here, a special dagger he created just for the halfbloods. Aadi is free to end his torment any time he wishes. When he does, his spirit will join the other halfbloods inside the dagger who have killed themselves with it. You see, Taral, Aadi won't be alone or empty anymore. The end to his pain is only one knife thrust away. Aadi is free to keep living as he wants or to end his life if he wishes. And the king has taken Aadi as his personal servant, giving him meaningful work to do as long as he wishes to stay with us." Lord Jesson paused. "Of course, he may not continue as His Majesty's servant for long, he's grown too weak to do much of anything at all these days. He's quite mad."

Aadi leaned his head back against the bare stone and closed his eyes. The truth sent shivers through him. His greatest fear was true; he was a halfblood like Kumar Raza. He would never be able to bond.

"Well, if His Majesty is through with the boy, perhaps he will give him to me." Lord Taral's voice held an unaccustomed cold edge to it.

"Perhaps," Lord Jesson said. "Come, we'll go ask him."

The two Naga Lords left the room, and Aadi crawled out from behind the tapestry. What do I do, he thought, what do I do?

Join us. The ghosts from the dagger swirled around him, tickling the back of his neck and brushing up against his face and arms. *Join us. End your pain.*

Aadi shook his head, but could not stop the whispers that filled his mind. He did not know how long he sat frozen there with the dagger in his hand and the world spinning in black emptiness. The tip of the dagger inched closer and closer to his chest.

"Aadi." Lord Taral's bright voice startled Aadi, and he dropped the dagger. It clattered to the ground, and he stared at it, unable to tear his gaze away from the beating silver heart clutched in the dragon's claws.

Lord Taral snatched up the dagger, hissed in surprise, and dropped it. "By the fountain." He shook his hand off as if he'd just sunk it into a pile of camdor droppings. Catching sight of the box on the floor by the tapestry, Lord Taral picked it up. After examining it for a moment, he set it down next to the dagger, and used the toe of his boot to flick the blade inside.

Aadi kept his head down. When Lord Taral closed the lid and fastened the catch, Aadi wanted to protest that the dagger was his, and Taral had no right to take it from him, but he didn't have the strength left to speak.

Lord Taral tucked the box away in his own robes and ordered Aadi to get to his feet.

Aadi tried, but his legs gave out, and he collapsed back in a heap on the floor.

"You really are worthless." There was that edge to Lord Taral's voice again. "*Get up!*"

He grabbed hold of Aadi's mind and forced him to his feet with the power of the command. "*Come.*"

He dragged Aadi to the open chamber where Taral's dragon, Saanjh, waited. "Time to go home," Lord Taral said. "Lift him onto your neck, Saanjh. There's no chance he'll get there on his own."

The dragon picked Aadi up and set him on his neck behind his head. Lord Taral climbed on behind Aadi and held him in place like he had when he'd first brought Aadi to the palace. Only this time there were no comforting words from Lord Taral. Only the echoing thought rolling over and over again through Taral's mind. *Useless halfblood.*

The dragon flew over the city. Looking down, Aadi realized much of it had been completed. It was indeed, clean and bright and beautiful. People bustled through the wide streets. Sunlight glinted off the spacious homes. How long have I been here? Aadi thought. How long have I been dying every day and still left alive to suffer? He was answered only by the vast emptiness inside him.

Saanjh circled down to land in the courtyard of a mansion beside the river. Clear water sparkled in the sunlight. Aadi vaguely remembered Kumar Raza asking Parmver why the river had been dark and putrid and nothing would grow beside it. That had been after Kumar Raza and Devaj had come to visit the fountain. The river had changed now, the water was like crystal, and farmland flourished out beyond the city.

Saanjh lifted Aadi down from his neck. Aadi crawled over to the river and reached down into the water. "The river is healed?" Aadi murmured.

"King Devaj restored the fountain," Lord Taral said. "Come away from the water, Aadi."

Aadi lay on his stomach and plunged both hands into the cold current. There was something important about the river he knew, but he couldn't remember what. Taking a deep breath, he pulled himself forward, intending to roll into the water.

"No." Lord Taral grabbed the back of his shirt and jerked him to his feet. "You will not kill yourself. Do you hear me?" he shook Aadi hard, as if the rattling would force him to obey.

"Come on." Lord Taral dragged him into the mansion and down the hall to a large sleep chamber. He pushed Aadi onto the bed then put his hands on his hips and stared at him. His eyes were so cold and angry that Aadi cringed away, crawling across the bed to drop down on the floor behind. He pressed himself flat and tried to pretend he did not exist.

"Giri," Lord Taral shouted.

An elderly human man hurried in and bowed. Aadi watched him across the space under the bed. "Yes, My Lord?"

"There's a young man here."

"There is?" Giri glanced around the room.

"He's hiding behind the bed. He's been very ill. I want you to take care of him. Get him a bath and some clean clothes. Comb his hair out, for goodness sake, and put him to bed. Force him to eat something, even if it is only a little. He's not in his right mind, so pay no attention to his ramblings. Send for some of that medicine to kill pain and help a man sleep. I'll be back as soon as possible."

Lord Taral strode out of the room, leaving Aadi alone with Giri. Aadi shuddered as the old man stepped around the bed to look at him. "Well, you are a mess," Giri said.

He swept off to an adjoining chamber, and Aadi heard water running into a tub. Giri came back, drying his hands on a towel. "Thank the fountain they got the plumbing working. Saves me a lot of heavy lifting."

He leaned down and put a hand on Aadi's arm to raise him to his feet.

Aadi pulled away and dragged himself under the bed where he curled into a ball. "I'm a halfblood. I'm a halfblood. I'm a halfblood." Every time he repeated it, his mind argued back. No, I'm a Naga. I'm a Naga. He screamed and dug his fingernails into the flesh of his arms, scratching and tearing as if he could tear away the human half of him to let the Naga part free.

Giri got down on his knees, grabbed Aadi's leg, and pulled him out from under the bed. Aadi thrashed to get away. His boot struck Giri's face, and Giri released him. "You *are* mad," Giri said putting his hand to his jaw. "I don't know how his Lordship thinks I can handle you."

Giri left Aadi panting and came back with three strong stonemasons. The men dragged him up, stripped his clothes off him, and held him in the tub while Giri washed him. Then they got a nightshirt on him and flung him down on the bed.

"Bind his hands and feet so he doesn't hurt himself anymore," Giri told them. He handed the men leather straps which, despite Aadi's desperate attempt to get away, they used to bind Aadi's wrists and ankles to the bedposts.

Giri thanked his helpers and let them go. He approached the bed and stared down at Aadi, his eyes troubled. "What does His Lordship want with you, I wonder? I know he's accustomed to taking in strays and nursing them back to health, but I don't see what he can do for you."

Aadi barely heard him. Though he no longer carried the dagger, the world had returned to muted grays and blacks, darker now than before. All he knew was pain and emptiness. At least before he'd had the hope that he would someday bond and end his agony.

"Are you hungry?" Giri tucked some pillows behind his back and head, positioning him more upright. "His Lordships wants you to eat."

Aadi shook his head. What good would food do? It could not ease the hunger inside him.

Giri frowned and lifted a cup of warm broth to Aadi's lips. Aadi pressed his lips closed and refused to drink.

"Being difficult won't help you. I am not accustomed to failing any task His Lordship has set me." He dug his fingers into Aadi's jaws, prying his mouth open, and forcing the broth down his ragged throat. When the cup was empty, he got a cloth and wiped Aadi clean of all that had spilled in the process.

Aadi lay back, panting, wishing he could get his hands back on the dagger. If he ever held it again, he knew he would hesitate no longer. He would give anything to join the other halfbloods who had been his only companions for so long.

Giri got a comb and raked at Aadi's hair until the snarls pulled free. When he left, Aadi thrashed against the straps that held him, trying to free himself. If he could not have the knife, there was always the river just outside. Drowning would be easy enough.

Chapter Thirteen

Giri returned a while later with a small glass decanter filled with a brownish liquid. He sat down next to Aadi. "You need to drink this, lad."

Aadi panted, too weak to speak or fight any longer.

"Are we going to do this the easy way or the hard way?"

Aadi let out an anguished cry.

Giri pressed a warm hand against his chest. "I know you're hurting. I can see that. But this is medicine to ease the pain. You need only take a couple of swallows." He moved the decanter to Aadi's lips.

"Hold on." Lord Taral strode into the room. He had a leather satchel at his side and a small plate of raw minced meat in his hand. He set the plate down on the bedside table, caught sight of Aadi, and flushed. "What happened? What did you do to him, Giri?"

"What did I do to him?" Giri put a hand to his bruise-darkened jaw.

"What?" Lord Taral turned Giri's head so he could get a better look. "Oh, for goodness sake. What happened?"

"He's mad," Giri said. "Utterly insane. All I did was try to help him up, and he kicked me."

"What happened to his arms? Why did you tie him down?"

"Those scratches? He did that to himself. I had to get three strong men in here just to get him bathed and in bed. We had to tie him. He would not stop trying to harm himself." Giri held up the decanter. "But I've got the medicine now. It should put him to sleep, though I think a better solution would be for you to use your powers to set his mind straight. No offense, My Lord, but it seems to me, some Naga Lord, your brother perhaps, has gone a bit too heavy with their powers and shattered his mind."

"How dare you?" Lord Taral's voice turned so hard and angry it made Aadi gasp.

Giri stepped back in fright as if Lord Taral had never spoken to him like that before. His hand shook on the decanter, nearly spilling the medicine.

"Give me that." Lord Taral snatched it from him. "The boy's madness is the fault of Kanvar and the other traitors who murdered King Amar. They did this to him, not my brother."

Giri dropped to his knees and bowed his head. "Forgive me, My Lord."

Lord Taral sucked in a deep breath and waited to the count of three before speaking again. "Giri. Thank you for tending to him. If I could heal his mind, believe me, I would. You may go and attend to your other duties now."

"Thank you, My Lord." Giri got to his feet and backed out of the room, then turned and fled.

Lord Taral turned his attention on Aadi.

Aadi squeezed his eyes closed and pressed himself against the bed, wishing he could disappear. His wrists and ankles stung where the leather had chaffed him as he tried to escape. Lord Taral was the only one since he'd come to Varna that had been nice to him, and now even Taral had turned against him. "Let me die," Aadi whispered. "Please give me the dagger back. It was a present from the king. You have no right to take it."

"Aadi," Lord Taral's voice was softer but still strained. "I have brought you a different present in exchange for the dagger. One you'll like better, I think." He set the decanter down and drew out a small bundle of cloth from the satchel. A mewling sound came from within.

Lord Taral laid the bundle in Aadi's lap and eased aside the cloth. Curled inside the fabric was a kitrat hatchling. Its gray scales pulsed in time with its breathing, and its black eyes blinked up at Aadi.

Aadi sucked in a breath. The kitrat's presence was like a tiny pinprick of light in his darkened mind.

"Here." Lord Taral freed Aadi's right hand.

Aadi shook off the leather strap and gently stroked the kitrat. The kitrat responded with a purr and wrapped itself around his hand, holding on tight with tiny claws.

"His mother's dead," Lord Taral said. "Along with the rest of the clutch. Smashed by a falling stone, but he survived. Though he won't live for long without someone to care for him. The mother keeps the young kitrats close to her for safety. They ride on her back and chest whenever she leaves the nest. They can't chew their own food yet. She has to chew it for them. There is very little chance this hatchling will survive without her unless . . ." Lord Taral released Aadi's other hand. "Unless you take the place of its mother."

Aadi looked up at Taral. "How . . . how can I?"

"Here, I'll show you." Lord Taral picked up a piece of the finely-minced meat. "The mother licks the edges of his mouth to tell him it's time to eat." Lord Taral rubbed the small piece of raw meat along the outside of the kitrat's mouth. After a moment of Taral's rubbing, the kitrat opened its jaws, and Lord Taral shoved the meat inside. The kitrat closed and swallowed, then opened its mouth again, mewling for more. "Your turn." Lord Taral handed Aadi a piece of the meat and motioned for him to go ahead.

Shaking and weak, Aadi pressed the food into the kitrat's open mouth. The kitrat accepted the meat, licked its lips, and looked up expectantly at Aadi for more. Lord Taral moved the plate of meat down onto the bed where

Aadi could reach it without straining. "They don't eat much at a time, so you'll have to feed him often. In a few days or so, you should be able to get him to eat directly off the plate and lick water from a bowl, but he's not strong enough for that yet." Lord Taral pulled out a dropper, filled it with water, and rubbed the tip along the kitrat's mouth until he opened up again to take the drink Taral squeezed out.

"Caring for a kitrat hatchling is a lot of work, and I know you don't have a lot of strength right now," Lord Taral said. "But, if you can keep this hatchling alive, help it grow strong, and you grow stronger along with it, I'll get you a camdor hatchling to raise and train."

"But." Aadi blinked back tears. "I killed the last camdor you gave me. Jenna's dead." Aadi had been trying not to think about Jenna for a long time, but now the emptiness of her loss swept back over him.

"Jenna's death was not your fault, Aadi. In fact, you are a hero. You saved thousands of people. I could not be happier with you, or prouder."

"No." Aadi tensed and shook his head. "I've seen your eyes. Heard your voice. Felt your anger. I'm not a hero. I'm just a useless halfblood like you've been thinking over and over again. Useless halfblood. You've been so angry with me."

"No." Lord Taral's shields went up hard and strong, blocking Aadi from every aspect of his mind. "I'm not angry with you. I'm . . . no, that's treason. Just be quiet for a moment. Let me think." Lord Taral pulled away from Aadi and paced the room.

"I don't understand," Aadi whispered. The kitrat hatchling, having eaten and drunk its fill, climbed up Aadi's arm to his chest and curled up beneath his nightshirt.

Lord Taral leaned against the wall and ran his fingers through his hair. "How can I say this?" He clenched his fists and tightened his shields even more. Silence hung in the room for a moment before he spoke again. "When a man plants an apple tree, he expects to get apples from it. If he allows a thorn bush to grow, he can expect to get punctured by the thorns. Apples do not grow on thorn bushes, and thorns do not grow on apples trees." Lord Taral closed his eyes for a moment and took a deep breath. "But I have seen thorns on the apple tree, Aadi, and I don't know what to do."

Aadi pressed his hands gently against the scaly bundle on his chest. He was still so alone and empty and yet not alone. Lord Taral had given him a most precious gift. Aadi did not like to see Lord Taral troubled. At first Aadi's tormented mind could not understand why Lord Taral was talking about apples and thorns, but gradually he thought he understood.

"You . . . finally believe me that King Khalid—"

"Silence, Aadi," Lord Tarral interrupted. "Don't say it. Don't even think it. Do you want to get me executed for treason?"

"Khalid knows what I think of him."

Lord Taral's face hardened and his eyes went cold. "But he doesn't know I think any such thing." Lord Taral grabbed Aadi's hands and refastened the leather straps around his wrists, tightening them and the ones on his ankles so he couldn't move at all. "To get him to let me have you, I had to make him believe that I would enjoy your torment, that I would prolong it, and take careful notes of every experiment I performed on you. I'm sorry, Aadi. I'm doing what I can to help you, but my allegiance lies with the king. I cannot cross him."

Lord Taral clenched his fists and paced the room again. "If only Kanvar hadn't betrayed and murdered King Amar we wouldn't have to face this nightmare."

Aadi swallowed a lump in his throat. "Kanvar didn't betray the king. I know, I was there."

"What?" Lord Taral turned to face Aadi, a stormy, tormented look in his eyes.

"King Amar's own dragon betrayed him. Khalid twisted Rajahansa's mind, perverted it with lies, and arranged all the events that led to Rajahansa's death. That was his plan from the beginning, to keep all the Nagas and humans focused on stopping Rajahansa so Khalid could force Devaj to Stonefountain and seize his body for himself. Khalid isn't here to help Devaj. He's taken Devaj prisoner in his own body and enslaved Devaj's dragon. Poor Elkatran. I saw him at the palace. Khalid has shattered his mind."

"Stop, stop. Be quiet." All light and hope vanished from Lord Taral's eyes. He slumped onto a chair and put his head in his hands. "We are lost."

Aadi did not like to see the hope leave Lord Taral's mind. It had been Lord Taral's hope and faith that had comforted Aadi while crossing with the caravan. "My Lord."

"Silence. You will not speak of this again. Not one word. Two of the Naga Guardsmen have already been beheaded for treason, and I'm not ready to die. What good would my death do? Nothing can stop King Khalid now."

"My Lord." Aadi glanced down at the lump under his nightshirt. "You have given me a gift, and I'd like to give you one in return. Since you have forbidden me to speak, I beg you to look into my mind. I know it's a painful, uncomfortable place at the moment, but I'd like to show you something."

Lord Taral raised his head to look at Aadi. "It would probably have been more merciful for me to let you kill yourself."

"Then let me do it. After you accept my gift. Come on. I promise I won't hurt you. How could I, I'm only a halfblood. I'll share a single image. I don't think that is treason."

Lord Taral got to his feet and came over to the bed. "Are you sure?"

"Trust me. You've done more for me than anyone else. Let me pay you back."

Taking a deep breath, Lord Taral eased his hand down on Aadi's forehead.

Aadi forced his sickened mind to draw up one image from the past. One single image—that of King Amar standing beside Bensharie, his hand on the young dragon's shoulder. Both had matching scars, terrible scars. *King Amar is alive*, Aadi said in his mind. *Though the dragon that betrayed him perished, King Amar has rebonded to this young one. Bensharie is a good companion.*

Lord Taral jerked his hand back and stumbled away from the bed. "By the fountain, what do I do?"

"You could ask him that," Aadi said. "I know his mind well. I'm not strong enough to reach him at this distance, but I think, perhaps, you are."

Lord Taral shook his head. "I couldn't presume to do such a thing. I'm no one of importance. Just a regular guardsman. I'm not even allowed into the king's presence without the escort of the Elite Guard."

"My Lord." Aadi shifted, uncomfortable with the straps that held him bound. "King Amar has no such rules. Anyone who wishes to visit is welcome. He receives them with pleasure."

Lord Taral came back and went to his knees beside the bed. A spark of hope rekindled in his eyes. "You think he would not be angry? This wouldn't be like a normal audience. I'd be intruding directly on his mind. That is discourteous even for another guardsman, let alone a king."

"I'm close to the king, My Lord, a descendant, mixed with other Naga and human blood, but a descendant all the same. He treats me like a son. He gave himself into the hands of enemies in exchange for my life. He will not mind you helping me contact him."

"All right." Lord Taral smoothed the sweaty hair back from Aadi's face. "But, you may be too weak for this."

"I think you should try," Aadi said. "That way even if I die, you at least will have something to live for."

Lord Taral pressed his hand to Aadi's head, and Taral's mind, like a gentle ray of morning sunrise, spread across Aadi's. Aadi sucked in a breath. With Lord Taral fully inside his mind, the emptiness slunk back. Lord Taral, with complete control and courtesy, left all of Aadi's memories and perceptions alone save one, Aadi's ability to feel King Amar's presence. Lord Taral absorbed that, but with the great distance and all the living creatures in the world to search among for the king, Lord Taral could not find him.

Aadi panicked, but Lord Taral soothed his fear. *It's all right, Aadi. I need just a little more information is all. Please picture the last place you saw him and share with me the sense of the other minds that are likely to be around him.*

Panting, Aadi tried to focus. Though Lord Taral was gentle and gave Aadi his privacy, Aadi's anxiety increased. Lord Taral pulled away, abandoning Aadi's mind. The emptiness washed back over him like a wave of sharp daggers, rending his heart. He screamed and thrashed against his bonds.

"I see you're doing a good job with him." Khalid's voice startled Aadi into silence.

Through his dark agony, Aadi saw that Elkatran had landed outside, and Khalid had entered the house and now stood in the doorway. Lord Taral snapped his shields tight around his own mind and whirled around to face Khalid.

"Your Majesty." Lord Taral dropped to one knee and bowed his head.

Khalid strode into the room and circled the bed. Aadi whimpered.

"You took the dagger and gave him a kitrat in its place like we discussed?" Khalid asked.

"Yes, Your Majesty."

"And the outcome?"

"It has only made him worse. He's been begging me for the dagger. He tried to drown himself in the river, and well . . . his arms. You can see what he's done to himself. I had to bind him. I imagine I'll have to keep him bound from now on if I'm to continue with the experiment as you requested."

Aadi moaned and thrashed at his bonds. "Let me die. Let me die. Your Majesty, please. Why didn't you tell me I could never bond?"

"Because I find your pain amusing." Khalid rested a hand on Aadi's forehead.

Aadi retreated deep within himself, putting all his strength and will into a shield, and burying that behind a wall of his empty pain and madness. If Khalid found out what Lord Taral had really been doing, Taral's life would be forfeit.

"Because you believed you were a Naga," Khalid said, "you have far outlived any other halfblood I have experimented on. How did you come to learn the truth?" Fingers of black snaked into Aadi's mind, probing his thoughts

"It was an unfortunate twist of fate," Lord Taral said, halting Khalid's advance into Aadi's mind. "It seems Aadi was hiding in the chamber Lord Jesson drew me into to explain Aadi's condition in secret. After gaining your permission to experiment on him, I found him there, a breath away from killing himself. I don't think he will ever forgive me for forcing the knife from his hand. It's rather amusing, really."

Khalid laughed and stepped away from the bed. "I like you, Taral. Come up to the palace tomorrow, and I will raise you into the Elite Guard."

Aadi shuddered. If Lord Taral were drawn that close to Khalid, the king would sense Taral's doubts and execute him as a traitor.

"Your Majesty. I am honored," Lord Taral said.

"Indeed you should be." Khalid strode to the door. "We will speak again tomorrow." Khalid took his leave of them, and Aadi hardly dared breathe until he felt Khalid's presence enter the palace far above.

Lord Taral stood a long time with fists clenched and gritted teeth before speaking. "I'm sorry I hurt you, Aadi."

"You didn't hurt me," Aadi said through trembling lips. "It was only the shock of you leaving my mind. Though it was a good thing you appeared to have hurt me at that moment."

"Yes, indeed." Lord Taral returned to the bed and sat down beside Aadi. "But it seems your mind is too hurt at the moment for me to use to try and speak with His Majesty Amar."

"It's not going to get any better," Aadi said. "You are just being too nice. If I can't control my thoughts enough to give you what you need, you're just going to have to go in and take it. Look through my mind, find the memories and feelings you need, and use them."

Lord Taral grimaced. "I cannot invade your privacy in such a way."

"It is not an invasion if I give you permission. My Lord, I want to speak with the king. I need to tell him farewell before I die. Please, help me to do so, even if that means some discomfort for you."

"You don't have to die, Aadi." Lord Taral stroked the kitrat curled up on Aadi's chest. "You don't have to be alone. You have this kitrat, and I have promised you another camdor. I know your connection to the lesser dragons is not the same as a full bond with a Great Gold, but it is something. You were happy with Jenna, remember?"

Aadi nodded.

"Do you still want me to help you contact King Amar, even if it means I enter areas of your mind that are private?"

"Please." Aadi nodded again.

"Then I will do it, but I hope His Majesty Amar does not take offense." Lord Taral pressed his hand against Aadi's forehead, and light returned to Aadi's mind. But Lord Taral was more forceful this time, pressing back the pain and delving deep into Aadi's memories. He sucked in and analyzed every aspect of Aadi's life, living with him the joy of his childhood growing up in the palace, the frustration he'd felt with Kanvar for refusing to dress right for his Choosing Ceremony, the anxiety he felt as the Nagas at the palace splintered and contention rose up between them culminating with King Amar being chained in his own room, and everything that followed after. Once Lord Taral understood the full essence of Aadi's life, his connection to King Amar, and the place King Amar was likely to be at that moment, Lord Taral turned his thoughts outward, seeking the king. He found King Amar standing on the edge of a village platform with Bensharie, discussing his concern for those he'd sent out to build an army strong enough to combat Khalid. He'd heard nothing from anyone recently, and it concerned him.

My King? Lord Taral said, brushing gently against Amar's mind to get his attention.

Aadi! King Amar's thoughts snapped into connection with Aadi's and Taral's.

Aadi, awash in the grief of the truth that he would never be able to bond, found himself unable to answer. Lord Taral spoke for him. *Aadi is mortally hurt. I am doing everything I can to keep him alive, but I fear it might not be enough. He asked me to contact you so he could say goodbye.*

No, it can't be. Who are you? What has happened? King Amar's joy at being in contact with Aadi vanished in fear and worry.

My King, Lord Taral said. *My name is Taral. Aadi is a halfblood and can never bond. Khalid has been tormenting him. I am only a lowly guardsman, but I have convinced Khalid to let me care for Aadi now that he has grown too weak for Khalid to do anything more with him. Aadi has shared with me the truth of what happened in Kundiland and the knowledge that you are alive. I would serve you, but two others have already been executed for having the least thought or emotion Khalid sensed as a betrayal. Our position is precarious. What do you want me to do? Whatever it is, whatever the danger, I'll do it.*

Without answering Lord Taral, Amar turned his focus to Aadi. His thoughts were gentle and filled with love. *Aadi, I'm sorry. This is a hard blow, a heavy burden for you who had such a bright vision and hope of how your life would be when you bonded with a Great Gold dragon. But this does not need to be the end for you. You don't have to give in to your grief. Kumar Raza hasn't. Though he is at times jealous of his brother, he still lives to serve me, and you can't deny his greatness. And you are just as great, Aadi, just as important. King Khalid may not value a halfblood any more than a cripple, but I do. You are as dear to me as Kanvar. Do you suppose it is easy for Kanvar to live with a crippled body? No, it is hard. It is painful, but that does not stop him from serving me. Perhaps you are crippled like Kanvar, though your infirmity is not one others can see. Physically, he is half a man. Spiritually you are missing your other half as well. But do not let that stop you. Promise me, Aadi, you will fight to stay alive.*

Your Majesty, I can't, Aadi whimpered.

Yes, you can. Now rest, and let me talk to Lord Taral. We have much to discuss.

Aadi gave control of his thoughts back to Lord Taral and let his sense of self fade back into the emptiness that consumed him. Lord Taral and Amar spoke for a long time, most of it Aadi was too weak to listen to. He understood only that King Amar asked Taral to find other Nagas who could see Khalid's evil and wished to join Amar. It seemed vitally important that there be enough Nagas inside the city to free the minds of the human soldiers from Khalid at the right time. King Amar knew it was a dangerous and seemingly impossible task, but Lord Taral agreed to do it. He swore an oath to Amar's service with all his heart.

Goodbye for now, Aadi, Amar spoke to him again. *I expect to see you alive and well soon. Don't disappoint me.*

Aadi made no attempt to answer. Khalid had burned away all desire to survive. King Amar's mind vanished from his own, and Lord Taral withdrew as well, slowly this time, easing out of Aadi's mind but leaving behind a light sense of his presence so as not to drop Aadi back into abrupt emptiness like he had done before.

Aadi blinked as awareness of the room around him returned.

Lord Taral left the room and returned with the silver box that housed the halfblood dagger.

Aadi drew himself up the best he could with his bonds. Anticipation flooded through him.

"No, Aadi," Lord Taral said. "This isn't for you. King Amar has asked me to do something with it. You can come with me if you like, or I can leave you here." Lord Taral frowned and glanced out the window toward the palace. "It's dangerous. We could be caught and killed."

"I welcome death," Aadi said.

"That's unkind." Lord Taral crossed to the bed, freed Aadi from his bonds, and drew him to his feet. "If you die, the baby kitrat will die as well."

Lord Taral eased the kitrat from beneath Aadi's nightshirt and tucked it, along with its food and water, inside the satchel he'd used to bring the kitrat home. Then he got clothes for Aadi and made him dress.

Aadi did not protest. With the satchel over his shoulder and the presence of the kitrat as well as Lord Taral in his mind, he felt a bit stronger. He could stand, at least, and breathe. He even felt the slightest stirring of hunger. Lord Taral went to the kitchen and brought him back some sweetbread and ham, which Aadi ate as they walked out to the courtyard beside the river. Darkness had fallen. It was a moonless night, but the stars blazed like diamonds in the sky, and lights spread across the city, reflected their glory. Storm clouds brooded on the northeastern horizon. Lord Taral and Aadi mounted Saanjh, and the dragon swept into the sky, flying toward the palace.

Chapter Fourteen

Saanjh landed in an empty courtyard that had not yet been rebuilt. Fallen stones and dust littered the ground. Here there were no sparkling lanterns or merry torches to push back the night. Lord Taral dismounted and helped Aadi down beside him.

"Wish us luck," he whispered to Saanjh.

Saanjh rumbled softly in response.

"Come, Aadi." Lord Taral drew Aadi out of the courtyard into a rubble-strewn hall. They picked their way carefully in the darkness until they came to where the palace had been rebuilt. Light gleamed from under the door.

"Aadi," Lord Taral whispered. "You've been in the palace for quite some time. You know its chambers and corridors. You've seen where the guards are stationed. I need to enter your mind now to see it all so we can navigate our way without being caught. May I?"

Aadi nodded. He felt at peace whenever Lord Taral joined him.

"Good lad." Lord Taral expanded his presence in Aadi's mind. Drawing on Aadi's experience inside the palace, he moved softly and confidently through the halls, avoiding anywhere the Elite Guardsmen were likely to be. He made his way to the central courtyard where the waters of Stonefountain flowed out of the mountain and dropped over the edge to fall in a torrent far down into the river below. The courtyard was lit with torches, and a half dozen human guards kept watch.

You do not see anything, Lord Taral whispered into their minds. *All is normal here, all is right. The courtyard is empty.*

The guards made no move or sound as Lord Taral took Aadi across the courtyard to a hall that led inward. *We're lucky there were no Nagas guarding the fountain tonight,* Lord Taral thought to Aadi as they entered the reconstructed hall leading to the fountain. *I guess Khalid has no fear of anyone taking stones from the fountain. He can just summon them back if he likes.*

Have we come to get singing stones? Aadi asked.

No, His Majesty Amar has forbidden me to disturb the stones of the fountain.

They stepped into a chamber aglow with a rainbow of pastel light. A sweeping song of joy caressed Aadi's mind. He could not hear the words of the song, but he could feel it, and it took his breath away.

Stay here and keep watch. Lord Taral left Aadi in the doorway and strode to the fountain. The sparkling water bubbled up from the center, filling the basin and spilling out to flow in a stream, down into a conduit and out across the courtyard where the guards were. Thousands of crystal stones, which had once glowed with their companions on the walls of the chamber, now rested in the basin where Khalid had set them after summoning them home.

Aadi leaned against the doorframe and wondered at their exquisite beauty.

Lord Taral pulled out the silver box that housed the dagger, undid the clasp, and tipped the box toward the water.

"No." Aadi rushed forward, but Lord Taral caught him with a strong arm, holding him back as the dagger slid from the box and plunged into the fountain. Black wisps scattered from the dagger, turning gray, then pale white, then bursting into dazzling color before dissipating into the water. The song of the fountain intensified. A crackling sound pulled Aadi's attention to the wall, and he watched in amazement as new crystals grew in a bare patch left by Akshara's claws.

Water splashed, and Aadi realized Lord Taral had retrieved the dagger from the fountain. He locked it back in its silver case and tucked it away. "His Majesty will be pleased that worked," Lord Taral said.

Aadi went to the wall and brushed his fingers along the new crystals. He heard voices he recognized from the whispers of the dagger, only now they no longer whispered in vast loneliness, now they sang for joy as their spirits intertwined with all the others of the fountain. The half-bloods were no longer empty and alone, and Aadi longed to join them.

Lord Taral came to Aadi's side. "They are at peace now."

"Yes." Aadi's hand shook where it rested against the stones. "Please, let me join them. You know I will have no peace in life. If you won't let me use the dagger, then at least use your sword. Free me from this pain." Aadi dropped his hand toward Taral's sword.

"No." Taral grabbed his wrist. "You feel like you are alone, but you are not. I am with you, and you have many Naga and dragon friends, people who care about you. I have seen them in your mind. What about Indumauli? Did you not agree to meet him here at Stonefountain?"

"Indumauli." Aadi shivered. He'd forgotten about his friend. How could he? Had Indumauli made it to Stone-fountain, or died in the ocean? Had the salt water killed him?

"Indumauli!" Aadi cried out with his voice and mind.

"It was the compulsion put on your mind when you were taken that made you forget Indumauli," Lord Taral said. "It is always done that way. Those chosen to join the caravan were relieved of the burden of the memories of their loved ones in Daro so they would not mourn to leave them behind. I should have realized you'd forgotten him, but I was preoccupied talking with King Amar. I don't think you had any other friends in Daro though. All your other memories seem to be intact."

Aadi. Indumauli's mind snaked into Aadi's. *Stay there, I'm coming.*

"He's alive. He's coming," Aadi told Taral.

"Tell him not to. We'll meet somewhere else. It's too dangerous here." Taral moved across the chamber toward the exit.

Aadi relayed Taral's message to Indumauli, but Indumauli's mind became agitated. The impressions Aadi got from him were desperate. *No, no, stay there, I need you, I'm coming.*

Need me?

To talk to Rajahansa. Only the Nagas can hear and see the spirits, Indumauli said. Aadi could feel him swimming at top speed up the river.

"My Lord," Aadi said, moving to the far side of the fountain where Lord Taral couldn't grab him. Aadi put up his shields hoping he would be strong enough to resist Taral if Taral tried to take control of his mind.

"What are you doing?" Taral said. "Khalid will kill us if he finds us here. Or worse."

"Indumauli says to wait for him here. I will not leave without him."

Lord Taral grimaced but returned to the fountain. A while later, water splashed and Indumauli slithered out of the stream. Damp black coils enveloped Aadi, and Aadi realized Indumauli had climbed up the waterfall and slithered along the stream into the fountain chamber.

Aadi, Aadi, Indumauli said. *I've been trying to find you but have not been able to feel you or touch your mind at all. It's as if your presence has been blocked from me. Why didn't you call me?*

Aadi wrapped his arms around Indumauli's neck in a tight hug. "Indumauli, I'm so glad to see you."

"Greetings," Lord Taral said to Indumauli. "I see you succeeded in making your way around the continent and up the river to Stonefountain."

You know me? Indumauli said.

"I've seen you in Aadi's mind. I'm sorry he's been blocked from you, but I've repaired that now."

Indumauli hissed and snapped at Lord Taral. *His mind does not feel repaired to me. His heart is in agony. He has not yet bonded, and I know why. You and the rest of the filthy Naga Guardsmen have chained his friends in the cavern and left them to die!*

Aadi choked back a bitter sob. "It's not Lord Taral's fault I haven't bonded. Indumauli, I can't. I'm not a Naga." He shivered, fearing Indumauli would no longer wish to be his friend once he learned the truth about Aadi.

Lord Taral took a step toward Aadi. Indumauli hissed and snapped at him again, almost grazing his cheek with his poisonous fangs.

Lord Taral jumped back. "It is not safe to stay here, Great One. Aadi and I will be killed if we're discovered. Let Aadi go, and you can meet us back in the river at my courtyard."

Indumauli's coils tightened on Aadi.

"Lord Taral's a friend," Aadi said, but Indumauli refused to listen. Keeping Aadi wrapped in his coils, he slid him over to the fountain.

Find Rajahansa for me. I've come so far to speak with him. I need you to do this for me. Indumauli gently took hold of Aadi's hands and eased them into the fountain. Ghosts appeared in the water as his fingers rubbed the stones. *Speak to them*, Indumauli said. *Ask for Rajahansa.*

A streak of terror went through Aadi. He did not want to face Rajahansa again, but he knew he must. Indumauli had paid a high price in carrying Aadi across the ocean so he could find the gold dragons. The spirits swirled around his fingers. "If you please," Aadi said to them. "I need to talk to Rajahansa. Will you call him out for me?"

The spirits swirled in a lazy circle but made no response.

"They won't speak to me," Aadi told Indumauli. "I am a halfblood and they know it. I'm no use to you."

Indumauli released Aadi and caught up Taral in his coils, resting the tip of his poisoned fangs against Taral's throat. *Call Rajahansa for me.* He forced Taral up to the fountain where he could lower his hands into the water.

Lord Taral took control of Indumauli's mind, eased the fangs away from his throat, and forced Indumauli's body to uncoil from around him. "Why do you want to speak to Rajahansa?" Taral asked in a cold voice.

He was my king, Indumauli said, *and my friend. Things were not settled between us when he died.*

Lord Taral glared at Indumauli.

Aadi dropped to his knees before Taral. "Please, My Lord. What can it hurt?"

Lord Taral took in a slow breath. "Very well, I will do it for you, Aadi, because you saved the caravan for me." Taral eased his hands into the water and spoke for a long few minutes with the spirits. Aadi could not hear their words and only made out the general idea of the conversation. None of the spirits of Stonefountain knew Rajahansa. When he had died, his spirit had not come to Stonefountain. His resting place lay elsewhere, somewhere in Kundiland most likely.

Lord Taral withdrew his hands from the fountain and shook the water off them. "I'm sorry, Indumauli. If you seek Rajahansa, you will have to look for him in Kundiland."

Indumauli let out an angry hiss, grabbed Aadi up in his coils and dragged him down into the river, following the water through the conduit, across the courtyard and off the side of the mountain.

Aadi gasped for breath as he hit the open air. He had not been ready to be taken under water. "I hope you haven't drowned my kitrat," Aadi said as Indumauli spread his wingfins and launched into a glide that took Aadi away from the palace and down in a spiral to the base of the falls. They splashed into the water and dove. Indumauli pulled him under an iron grate across the entrance to a cave that led below the waterfall into the mountain. Indumauli surfaced beyond the grate and set Aadi up on a rock ledge that followed the course of the river.

Aadi pressed up against the rock wall and scrubbed his dripping hair out of his eyes. He opened his satchel, plunged his hand in, and drew out the cloth nest where the kitrat hatchling lay. The cloth was damp, but the thick leather had kept most of the water out. Aadi unwrapped the hatchling and pressed it up against this neck where his body could warm it. It made no sound, but Aadi could feel the faint movement of its breathing.

I'm sorry, Indumauli said. *I did not realize you had a friend with you.*

"Lord Taral is a friend as well," Aadi said. "You should not have threatened to bite him. He's working for King Amar."

That's pleasant news, but you must come quickly. Indumauli swam upriver, urging Aadi to follow. Keeping the kitrat safe against his warm skin, Aadi followed the ledge, feeling his way in the dark. "This is crazy. I can't see anything," he said.

Just a little farther, Indumauli reassured him, leading Aadi with his mind. *There's light up here, not much, but a little.*

Aadi rounded a curve in the river, and the way opened into a cavern. A single lamp burned on the wall on the far side near a passageway leading up. The flicker of orange flame did little to light the cavern.

Aadi.

An aching despair washed over Aadi, but he recognized Jaymon's voice in his mind. As with his communication with Indumauli, he couldn't make out the exact words, just the meaning behind it. His friend, Jaymon, was wretchedly weak, but excited to see Aadi.

Aadi cast his gaze over the black shadows in the chamber and saw that ten Great Gold dragons were chained to the stone walls. The chains were long enough they could reach the water and each other but no farther. The young gold dragons hunched in the chamber, their skin sunken against their bones—Jaymon, Bellori, Fulkshema, Affonaly and others of Aadi's friends. The chamber stank from mounds of uncleared dragon waste.

Aadi covered his nose and mouth with his hand, and ignoring his watering eyes, pressed into the chamber and went directly to Jaymon. He reached a hand toward the dragon then jerked back. Touching the gold dragons hurt him now. After the agony of the Choosing Ceremonies Khalid had forced him to endure, Aadi could not bring himself to do it.

"Jaymon," he said aloud. "What are you doing here? What happened?"

Jaymon roused himself enough to lift his head a fraction from the ground. *We rebelled and tried to fight Khalid. But we were not strong enough to resist his power. He chained us here and left us to die of starvation.* Jaymon licked his lips and shook his head in agitation.

That is not exactly what Khalid said, Fulkshema spoke up. *He told us we could kill and eat each other and that if we did that, he would free the last of us to survive.*

Bellori let out a wretched howl. *Like we would do that, like we ever could.*

We've been surviving on kitrats and other vermin that find their way in here, but it is not enough, Jaymon said. *Then Indumauli found us. He's been bringing us food, and we've grown a bit stronger.*

But I cannot free them. Indumauli circled. *I have tried everything. I even stole a hammer and chisel from a blacksmith shop in the city, but chip the rock however much I might, I cannot break the chains loose. They have been manipulated to be part of the stone itself.*

"If the chains cannot be broken, what can I possibly do?" Aadi looked around at his friends. None of them had fared better at Stonefountain than he had. It seemed Khalid's cruelty would kill them all.

Aadi. Jaymon lifted a foreclaw to touch Aadi's arm, but Aadi screamed and spun away so Jaymon could not touch him. Aadi dropped to his knees, shivering. He wanted to feel his friend, wanted to touch his dragonstone, wanted to be as close to Jaymon as they once had been, but he could take no more pain, no more torment. Bad things happened to his mind when he touched the gold dragons.

Indumauli, what's wrong with him? Jaymon asked.

I don't know, Indumauli said, his body coiling and uncoiling in agitation. He rubbed across Aadi's chest and back, careful not to crush the fragile kitrat in Aadi's hands. *Aadi, what's wrong? Talk to me, please. Your friends need your help.*

"What can I do? I have no power, and I never will. I am nothing but a wretched halfblood, but I will stay here and die with the rest of you, so you don't have to spend the last days of your life alone."

That's nonsense, Indumauli hissed. *Utter nonsense. None of you are going to die. Aadi, stop sniveling and listen for a moment.*

Ignoring Indumauli, Aadi emptied the water that had seeped into the satchel, wrung out the cloth, and reformed the kitrat's nest. Carefully, he eased the hatchling inside and closed the satchel.

Aadi. Indumauli brushed Aadi's face with the end of his tail. *Wake up. You have to free your friends. It doesn't matter right now whether you are a Naga or not. You have two feet and you can go where the rest of us can't. Khalid has the king's sword. Jaymon and the others say he wears it all the time.*

"Not when he's sleeping," Aadi mumbled.

Exactly. Indumauli hissed, his breath hot on the back of Aadi's neck. *It's nighttime now. He'll be sleeping. You have to take the passageway up into the palace, get the king's sword, and cut away the grate that blocks the entrance behind the waterfall. Then cut the chains, so your friends can fly away. We'll all go together and be gone from Stonefountain for good.*

Aadi sucked in a breath. His sluggish heart would not beat hard enough to give him the strength he needed. His mind was bleak, and death seemed the only end to his torment. But he looked around the chamber at his friends. Their suffering had perhaps been worse than his own. Sight of their starved and filthy bodies made him hurt along with them. He knew there could never be any end to his own torment, but Indumauli was right, the king's sword could free them. If he could get it.

Looping the satchel over his head and shoulder, Aadi got to his feet. Yet fear kept him in place. If he went up that passageway into the palace, he would have to face Khalid. The fountain willing, Khalid would be asleep and stay that way. But if Khalid woke and found the sword in Aadi's hands. Aadi shuddered. The things Khalid would do to him would be unspeakable.

Chains clanked as Jaymon drew himself to his feet and spoke to Indumauli. *Aadi is too frightened. Who knows what torment he has already faced at Khalid's hands. He can't do this, and we have no right to ask it of him. He'll be killed or worse. Indumauli, think for a moment. What would King Amar want us to do? The answer is obvious. You take Aadi and get him out of here. Take him back to Kundiland to the king. Our lives are of little value compared to his. In the name of the king, I order you to get Aadi out of here now.*

Indumauli hissed angrily.

Shivering, Aadi stumbled across the chamber toward the passageway. Jaymon was prepared to stay and die to save Aadi. Aadi could do no less for his friend. A single purpose solidified in Aadi's mind. He would get the sword, whatever it took, whatever dangers he faced, whatever punishments he'd receive. A life of freedom and joy awaited the young dragons outside this filthy pit. Aadi had no hope of that for himself, but he would do all in his power to guarantee it for his friends.

He knew his way to the king's chambers. The Naga Guardsmen were used to seeing him coming and going from the king's room. The ones on duty now would have been sleeping earlier in the day and may not know yet that Aadi had been given to Lord Taral.

No, Aadi. Stop, Jaymon said. The other dragons echoed his words.

Aadi paused beside the flickering oil lamp, his mind already forming a plan. "It's all right," he said. "I doubt Khalid can hurt me now any more than he already has. You can't begin to imagine what he's done to me, but it doesn't matter. I will free you from this prison."

Chapter Fifteen

Aadi crept up the passageway into the palace. All was quiet, every guard still at his post along the way to King Khalid's chambers. Aadi hoped that meant Lord Taral had gotten home without being discovered. Aadi kept his head down as he passed the Elite Naga Guardsmen. They ignored him as always as filth not even worthy of contempt.

Aadi slipped into his own servant's room and went through it into the king's chambers. There, he found Khalid asleep with a dagger clutched in his hand. Trusting no one, Khalid always slept like that. Elkatran hunched in the corner where he stayed unless Khalid ordered him to move elsewhere. Elkatran's eyes were open, but glossy. Aadi had no fear of the dragon giving him away. In all the time Aadi had been in the palace, Elkatran had never once acknowledged Aadi's presence. Aadi doubted there was anything left of Elkatran's mind.

While sleeping, King Khalid kept the sheathed Sword of the King hung on a display on the wall. A golden placard depicted Stonefountain, and the sword hung, blade down, in the center of the fountain, as if forever bathed in the water's power.

Muscles tense, Aadi eased the sword from its place. As he edged back the way he'd come, he noticed the Bonding Chalice still sitting out where Khalid had placed it in front of Aadi to taunt him. The golden cup was intricately wrought with dragons winding around it and a circle of glittering rubies below the outer rim. It was beautiful, and for so long Aadi had pinned all his hopes on someday drinking from it. He shook his head, knowing it was useless. He would never bond. He would never be a Naga. And still his hand reached for the chalice. What could it hurt to try? He'd found Jaymon at last. If he touched Jaymon's mind, perhaps Aadi would feel the pain he had felt with all the other gold dragons. But he'd felt that pain before and survived it. Jaymon and he were friends. Even if their minds could not link at Choosing, he was sure Jaymon would be willing to try for a bond anyway.

Hardly daring to breathe, Aadi wrapped his fingers around the cup and slipped it into the satchel at his side. Then he hurried back to his own chamber. There, as always, was a pile of bedding and clothing to be washed. While Aadi wrapped the sword in a bundle of laundry, he wondered who would do the work to keep up King

Khalid's chambers when he was gone. Lifting the bundle of clothes onto his back, Aadi stepped into the hall and hurried down toward the washing room.

In the lower halls of the palace, Aadi bypassed the washing room and continued back to the dark passageway that led down, down into the dismal chamber where the gold dragons waited. The smell once again assailed him, filling his nose and mouth. He choked and dropped the laundry bundle beneath the lamp.

Did you get it? Indumauli slithered out of the river and over to him.

"Yes." Aadi moved aside the clothes to reveal the sword. Its gold pommel glinted in the lamp light. Before lifting the sword, Aadi tore a strip of cloth from one of the shirts in the bundle and wrapped it around the sword's hilt, careful to keep his skin from brushing the weapon. He'd seen Liander flung across a palace chamber by a shock from the sword one day when he'd accidentally touched it.

But some of the king's blood does run in your veins, Indumauli said. *Parmver said he was sure of it when he took you to the palace.* Aadi knew King Amar had married two different village women. With the first, he had six children. Long after all those were dead, he married again and had seven more children. None of them had been Nagas, but King Amar's blood had flowed thick among the villagers ever since.

"As does Parmver's blood from his marriage with the villagers and a lot of other blood as well," Aadi said. "Even with the cloth shielding my hand from the hilt, I may not be able to wield this sword at all, but I'm going to try." He picked the sword up by the sheath and walked over to Jaymon.

Jaymon lifted a shackled foreclaw, holding his breath that Aadi would be able to cut him free.

Aadi knelt in front of his friend instead. "Jaymon, we have been friends for a long time. You were the first to greet me when I came to the palace as a little child. We have spoken often about bonding and had hoped, when the time came, the Choosing Ceremony would confirm the rightness we have previously felt with each other. Now, I have the dragon sickness but not the fever. Khalid insists I am a halfblood and cannot bond. My body is incapable of such a thing. He is most likely right. I daren't even touch your dragonstone as is custom for the Choosing Ceremony. I know from experience it will only cause me exquisite pain, though it probably wouldn't hurt you at all. But back in Kundiland, King Amar told me if I did not come down with the fever, I should try for a bond anyway." Aadi lifted the chalice out of the satchel and set it on the ground between himself and Jaymon. He tried to speak again, but a lump caught in his throat, and no more words came out.

Rumbling softly, Jaymon lowered his foreclaw to rest on Aadi's shoulder.

Aadi winced, but forced himself not to pull away. At Jaymon's touch, the empty pain inside Aadi intensified. He bit his lip, but couldn't stop the tremors that shook his body.

Even my touch hurts you? Jaymon murmured.

Aadi nodded, still unable to speak.

Jaymon pulled his foreclaw away. *This is a cruel, cruel thing. But King Amar is right. We should at least try for a bond that would ease your pain. I will attempt this bond with you, Aadi, if you will have me.*

"I want none other," Aadi said. "Let's just hope I can use this sword."

Gritting his teeth, Aadi curled his hand around the sword hilt. A shock like the prick of needles jolted his hand, but he was not thrown back, and though holding the sword was uncomfortable, he lifted it and used it to nick his own wrist, then Jaymon's. When the chalice was full, Jaymon licked both wounds closed.

Aadi set aside the sword, lifted the cup in his shaking hands, and held it out to Jaymon. "I dare not drink first. Who knows what it will do to me. This is all backwards and wrong. No Bonding Ceremony should take place in a putrid dungeon, in filthy damp clothes, without the presence of the king, but what else can we do? I'm frightened. You drink first."

Jaymon took the cup from Aadi's hand and drank his share. Aadi waited, shivering. He felt nothing but the emptiness that had become his only existence. Jaymon held the cup to Aadi's lips and waited.

Steeling himself, Aadi tipped his head back and drank. The mixed blood filled his mouth and slid down his throat, tasting cold and empty. After two swallows, his body convulsed. He bent double in pain and coughed and retched until there was nothing left in his stomach and throat. Even then he could not stop for some time. The most excruciating darkness spread over him, worse than any emptiness and pain he had experienced in the Choosing Ceremonies. He waited for himself to die. Surely no one could survive such agony. But death did not spread its loving arms to claim him. In all cruelty, it left him trapped among the living.

After some time, Aadi gasped and dragged his shaking body to his feet.

I'm sorry, Jaymon whispered.

Fighting the sting of tears, Aadi snatched up the sword and strode along the edge of the river to the cave's entrance where the metal grate blocked escape by flight. In anger spurred by his emptiness, Aadi hacked at the bars. The king's sword cut through them as easily as all else it was wielded against. Metal sparked, and the grate fell into the water and sank.

Aadi stalked back to his friends and hacked furiously at the chains that bound them. "Fly," he said as he released each one. "Fly for Kundiland. Don't slow down, and don't look back. If the Naga Guard catches you, all this will be for naught."

One-by-one the gold dragons zipped from the prison and out into the night.

Aadi came to Jaymon last. He took off the satchel and held it out. "My dear friend. Take this. Raise the kitrat hatchling for me. Lord Taral wants me to do it, but I haven't the strength."

Jaymon shook his golden head. "You are coming to Kundiland with me."

"You're too weak to carry me, Jaymon. You must fly at full speed if you're to have any chance of getting away. I'll follow you in the water with Indumauli. But the kitrat will drown. I can't keep it with me."

"You promise you'll come with Indumauli?" Jaymon lifted the satchel from Aadi's hands.

"I promise. Now go. And don't eat that kitrat, I've been tasked with saving its life, and I turn the task over to you." Aadi slashed the chains that bound Jaymon, setting him free. Just as the last chain rattled to the ground, the sword disappeared out of Aadi's hands.

Aadi, what are you doing with my sword? Khalid grabbed Aadi's mind and froze him in place.

"Fly, fly!" Aadi called out to Jaymon. At the same time Aadi fixed an image in his mind for Khalid to see—the impression of all the gold dragons still chained wretchedly in their places. Aadi believed that lie was true, believed it with all his heart, refusing to watch Jaymon take to the air, or hear the flutter of his wings as he zipped out of the cavern and made for Kundiland. Aadi had to convince Khalid the gold dragons were still in the chamber long enough for Jaymon and the others to get too far away for Khalid to take control of their minds.

Indumauli grabbed Aadi and dragged him toward the water.

"No, Indumauli," Aadi whispered. "I have to distract Khalid long enough for the others to get away. Go, hide, leave me, or we're all doomed."

Indumauli released Aadi and slid into the river.

Your Majesty. Aadi dropped to his knees in the presence of the king's mind. *I found my friends and wanted to try bonding.* Aadi lifted the chalice and twirled it so the rubies caught in the lamplight. Then he tipped it so Khalid could see the remains of the blood.

Khalid laughed. *And how did that work for you, Aadi?*

Aadi shuddered as Khalid raked through his mind for a sense of the depth of agony and anguish Aadi had experienced in his attempt to bond with Jaymon. What Khalid found there pleased him. *You should have stayed with Taral and his ridiculous kitrat. You are nothing but a halfblood, always have been, and always will be. It's too bad, but it is not I who chose your parentage. Stay right there. I am coming for you.*

Unable to move, Aadi stayed on his knees holding the chalice. His body hurt, and his soul was in agony, but at least his friends were getting away. He shielded thought from Khalid, keeping his head down and not looking at the empty chamber around him.

At last, Aadi heard footsteps in the passageway. He tensed and dropped the chalice as Khalid strode into the cavern.

"*What have you done?*" Khalid's cry of rage tore through Aadi, slamming him to the ground.

Khalid's boot fell on Aadi's chest, pinning him. Khalid's eyes, which usually glowed a soft gold, flared crimson. "How dare you!" Khalid lifted his sword to strike Aadi's head from his shoulders. But then he let out a ragged laugh and stopped. "You'd like that, wouldn't you? A swift painless end. No. I'll not grant you what you seek. I'm going to chain you here and let you live. Force you to eat and drink and live in agony forever."

Khalid grabbed Aadi's shirt and dragged him to the chains that had held Jaymon. Before he could manipulate the first in place around Aadi's wrist, Indumauli burst from the river and struck with his poisoned fangs at Khalid.

Khalid swung his sword in defense, dealing a blow that would have hit the top of Indumauli's head, cutting it in two if Aadi had not caught hold of his arm and diverted the blade.

Indumauli's dragonstone sparked as the sword cut through it then veered, flaying the skin from the side of his head instead of killing him. A piece of the dragonstone clattered to the ground beside Aadi. Though injured, Indumauli finished his strike, grazing Khalid's right arm with his fang. Aadi grabbed the shard of the dragonstone just as Indumauli's coils jerked him into the water.

Aadi threw up a shield around his mind and Indumauli's but knew Khalid could easily shatter his weak attempt and force both of them back to the surface. But Khalid was too busy swearing furiously as he cut the snake bite open and sucked out the venom. He had only moments to do so if he wanted to live. In that time, Indumauli raced out through the waterfall and downriver, dragging Aadi with him.

Indumauli only brought Aadi to the surface for air once or twice in his hurry to escape. Aadi felt for sure he was drowning, but didn't really care. His friends were free, that was all that mattered. Aadi had stood up to his tormentor, had tricked Khalid long enough for the young gold dragons to escape. Water rushed past Aadi's face as he gave up breathing. The river's currents were a welcome embrace to the end of his life.

Clutching the shard of Indumauli's dragonstone in his hands, a peace settled over Aadi. The tormenting emptiness faded. He was at home in the river with Indumauli. All seemed right for the first time since Haidar had slathered Aadi's skin with the burning ointment.

Indumauli turned from the main current of the river and swam into the lair he'd chosen several miles downriver from the city. Long ago a stately mansion had stood beside the river. The upper walls had long since fallen into heaps and been covered by sand and grown over by plants. But a section of the mansion's underground storerooms remained, partially flooded. Indumauli dragged Aadi out of the water onto the muddy shore.

Aadi stared blurry-eyed up at the dragon. Indumauli's head was bleeding. The wound stung, but Indumauli cared little for that at the moment. *Breathe, Aadi*, he said. Aadi closed his eyes. He cared nothing for breathing. He was with Indumauli; that was enough.

Breathe. Indumauli turned Aadi onto his side and pried his mouth open to get the water out of his throat. Aadi coughed the water out and took a breath. He felt no pain and figured death had come for him at last.

It's all right, Indumauli, he spoke into the serpent's mind. *Let me be. I'm at peace.*

Indumauli hissed in surprise and reared back. *Say that again.* Indumauli's command came into Aadi's mind in clear speech. His thoughts were sharp and focused.

Ouch, Aadi said. *You're head really hurts.*

Indumauli hissed in surprise and coiled around Aadi. *I can hear you, Aadi. I can hear your voice in my mind as clear as moonlight on the river.*

Aadi jolted to a sit. *I can hear you too. But how, we haven't bonded. We couldn't have.* Something cool and comforting pulsed in his hand. He opened his fist and saw the shard of Indumauli's dragonstone still clutched there.

"I think you lost something," Aadi said out loud.

Indumauli let out a hissing laugh. *No, I think I found something.*

"What?"

You, Aadi. You. I never dreamed I would be bound to a Naga someday, and yet here I am speaking to you, feeling your mind inside mine and my mind inside yours. Amazement and joy welled up inside Indumauli and spilled out into Aadi, filling him with joy as well.

"But I'm not a Naga," Aadi said. "I can't bond. What we're feeling can't be real."

Perhaps not in the sense that others have bonded, but you can't deny what we're feeling. I'm curious. Set the stone down for a moment. Indumauli moved back away from Aadi.

Aadi laid the shard of Indumauli's dragonstone on the muddy ground. An agonizing emptiness swept over him, and he lost contact with Indumauli's mind.

It is the dragonstone then. Indumauli's words were once again just vague impressions in Aadi's mind. Unable to stand the pain of his sudden loneliness, Aadi reached for the stone, but Indumauli picked it up first.

Just a moment. Indumauli examined the shard for a moment, then held it down against a stone, and bored a hole in it with one of his claws. A sharp pain stabbed through Aadi's mind and then vanished as Indumauli finished is work. *Pull the tie from your vest,* Indumauli instructed.

Getting the idea of what Indumauli intended, Aadi tore a tie loose from his vest and helped Indumauli thread it through the hole in the shard. When they finished, Indumauli draped the tie over Aadi's head and slid the piece of his dragonstone beneath Aadi's shirt. Aadi pressed the shard against his chest, and Indumauli's mind snapped back in full contact with his own. He breathed a sigh of relief and hugged Indumauli.

Indumauli hissed in appreciation of the bond he now felt with Aadi. He licked his bleeding head until the wound closed and neither of them felt any pain, just a peaceful comfort in each other's presence.

Aadi ran a hand down Indumauli's slick neck. "We did it. We freed the gold dragons. I fooled Khalid." Aadi laughed. "After all he did to me, I tricked him into thinking the gold dragons were still in the chamber while they escaped. Do you think they'll make it to safety?"

Indumauli let out a long soft hiss. *You gave them the best chance you could. If they're lucky, Khalid will be more focused on hunting us than hunting them.*

"By the fountain, I hope so." Aadi leaned back against Indumauli's coils and closed his eyes. "I'm sorry we did not find Rajahansa."

As am I. I just wanted to understand what could make my friend behave the way he did. I don't understand it. Rajahansa knew Khalid was evil, how could he believe his lies? An image of the beauty of the city of Stonefountain played across Indumauli's mind. *It is amazing what Khalid has done though. How can so much good come out of the heart of evil?*

Aadi swallowed. "I don't think Rajahansa could have answered that question for you, but I can tell you this, Khalid is a master at seeming to be all that is beautiful and wise in this world. He has fooled more than Rajahansa with his illusion of goodness and promise to restore the wonders of ancient civilization. By taking Devaj's body, he's been able to personify the very essence of gentleness and warmth. The Naga Guardsmen follow him because they believe he is a good man, and he is careful to make sure they keep believing it."

Indumauli hissed and wrapped comforting coils around Aadi. *Well, we know the truth.*

"Yes, we do. And somehow we will find a way to help King Amar stop Khalid." Aadi stroked the shard of the dragonstone that hung around his neck. Indumauli felt like so much a part of him that Aadi wondered why he had not recognized their connection before. "Indumauli, I . . . I think I'm glad I couldn't bond with Jaymon. If I had, I wouldn't be here with you. Do you think King Amar will be angry with us? I know Parmver would never approve."

Indumauli let out a rumbling purr. *I'm sure Rajahansa would be angry, but I don't care what Rajahansa thinks anymore. I know King Amar would not object to our bond, and I serve him now with all of my soul. You are right. We must help him find a way to bring down Khalid. But not now. Now, we need to stay hidden. The entire Naga Guard will be out looking for us by morning. Khalid will not forget or forgive my biting him.*

"We will stay here together then," Aadi said. Comfortable in the darkness with the black dragon, he drifted off to sleep.

About The Author

Rebecca Shelley (Rebecca Lyn Shelley) is the author of over 30 published books including the bestselling **Smart-boys Club** series as well as the popular **Red Dragon Codex** and **Brass Dragon Codex**. She loves writing about dragons and is excited to be writing the **Dragonbound** series. Her **Aos Si** *trilogy* will thrill fans of YA Paranormal Romance. To learn more or contact her, visit her website http://www.rebeccashelley.com.

If you have enjoyed reading **Dragonbound VIII: Black Dragon**, Rebecca would love to have you post a review on the site where you purchased it.

Dragonbound IX: Great Blue Liberator Preview
By Rebecca Shelley

Chapter One

Kanvar sat on Dharanidhar's back on a windswept beach. Clouds covered the moon, casting the heaving ocean waves in night-time shadows. Kanvar shivered in the cold wind and squinted across the water as the ships of Bolivar's fleet sailed away and disappeared. His sense of the people on the ships had vanished long before they boarded. No man, woman, or child, once made aware of their cause was allowed to remove their protective iron helmets. To Kanvar's mind, Bolivar's war fleet was unmanned, a ghost fleet sailing toward Varna, driven before the cold gale that whipped the water into monstrous waves.

Dharanidhar growled and tucked his wings tight against his body. Kanvar shifted in his leather saddle and double checked that the straps that held him in place were secure.

I agree, Dhar, but what can we do? Kanvar spoke into Dharanidhar's mind. *You and I both know better than to fly in a storm like this.* Both Kanvar and Dharanidhar were still living with the agonizing consequences of the last time they'd tried to fly across this ocean in a storm.

Lord Theodoric and Ishayu have gone with the fleet. Even LaShawn and Damodar are flying tonight. Surely if they don't fear to accompany the fleet, we can go too. Dharanidhar spread his wings, but the wind caught them in a forceful gust, and Dharanidhar had to strain to bring them back in to his sides. He growled in annoyance and sank to the sand.

Frost chirped in sympathy and flapped down to land on Dharanidhar's dragonstone. Kivi, who lay against Dhar's forehead as usual, snapped at Frost in annoyance.

"It's not fair," Denali said, climbing up Dharanidhar's foreleg to join Kanvar. "You're not the only one they left behind. I don't know why my father insists I'm too young to fight in this war. He let Raahi go with his father. I *can* fight, and you should see Frost in battle. She's unbeatable. And I don't understand why they had to leave at night, in this storm. It's like they're purposely trying to leave you behind. They can't even claim you're too young."

Kanvar clenched his good hand into a fist. "Kumar Raza, Stonebiter, Bolivar, and Theodoric know you and I can fight. That's not the problem. The problem is, how do you move an army without being seen by Bendyn and Weston? Those Naga guardsmen have gotten too close to discovering us on their own, and now they have reinforcements, ten more Nagas searching every mind of every person in every village and all of Huayna. It's like Khalid knows we're here and is trying to flush us out. The army had to move, and it's a sure bet the Naga guardsmen won't be flying tonight. This storm is the perfect opportunity to get away from Darvat unnoticed, and Bolivar's a good enough seaman he thinks he can ride it out. Dharanidhar and I will fly as soon as the wind dies down."

"You'd better take Frost and me with you."

"And leave Miki here by himself? Who will feed him and brush him and keep him out of mischief?" Kanvar asked.

"Raahi's mother will do it. I've already asked her. You know Tiago adores him."

Kanvar half smiled. Raahi's little brother, Tiago, had spent every moment he could with Kumar Raza's dog. "All right, you can come with us, Denali. But you realize Dhar and I are headed back to Kundiland, not to Varna? We have to harvest more herbs for his medicine before it's time to attack Stonefountain. He only has a few doses left."

"What? No. The jungle's too hot for Frost." Denali scowled.

"So is Varna, that's why Kumar Raza arranged for you to stay here with Raahi's mother. You may be grown enough to fight, but Frost is only a wyrmling. Even though she can fight, she's a baby, Denali. She needs to stay here where the climate is good for her."

Denali folded his arms across his chest. "Take us with you. To Kundiland if you must and then to Stonefountain."

Kanvar grimaced. "All right, but we're not going anywhere until the wind dies down."

Early morning gray streaked the sky as Lord Taral and Saanjh landed at the golden palace at Stonefountain. Taral's hands sweated, and if he'd let his fear run unchecked he and Saanjh would be headed back to Navgarod as fast as Saanjh could fly. They could probably hide for the rest of their lives in the wild mountains of Navgarod and never have to face King Khalid. But Taral had sworn himself into King Amar's service, and though he'd muddled it badly in losing Aadi, he couldn't abandon his other duties to the rightful king.

Striding as quickly as he could through the palace, he found Lord Jesson at his desk poring over reports. "My Lord," Taral said. "I hate to bother you so early in the morning. But I have news for the king that is most urgent. He'll be furious if I don't give it to him immediately. In fact—" Taral gritted his teeth. "He's going to be furious one way or another."

Lord Jesson gave Taral a rueful smile. "You can't begin to know how angry His Majesty is at you. He just told me to hunt you down and bring you to him."

Taral shuddered. "There is no need to hunt. I am loyal to the king and will accept whatever punishment he sees fit for my failures."

"Leave your sword here and come then." Lord Jesson unbuckled his own sword, laid it on the desk and motioned for Taral to do the same. Then he led Taral to the king's wing of the palace and let him into a reception chamber where King Khalid waited for him.

"Your Majesty," Taral dropped to his knees. "Aadi has vanished. Something tore him free of his bonds. I found a trail of water from the river to the room I where I held him. It looked as if some serpent came out of the river in the night, clawed him free, and dragged him down into the water. I could find no trace of him, no feel of his mind, nothing. I think he must be dead, drowned. Perhaps his mind was strong enough to summon the lesser serpent to end his life."

Stony faced, King Khalid lifted his arm to show a gruesome scar where there had not been one the day before. The skin around it was read and swollen. "Aadi is not dead. Not yet. He's working with a Great Black serpent from Kundiland."

Lord Taral's heart twisted with fear. Indumauli had struck the king. Whatever Indumauli and Aadi had been up to, Taral would be blamed and punished for it.

King Khalid's eyes narrowed, and he took a step toward Taral. "The serpent's name is Indumauli. He and that filthy halfblood have freed ten traitorous young gold dragons from my prison. Since the boy was in your care, I hold you responsible. You will make this right, Taral. I raise you to a member of the Elite Guard and task you with hunting them all down. Take whatever men and weapons you need. I want those dragons dead. I want their dragonstones spread before me. And I want the black serpent's hide nailed to my bedroom wall. But I want Aadi alive. Bring him to me so I can prolong his pain and madness forever."

"Yes, Your Majesty," Lord Taral said. "It is an honor to serve. I will bring these traitors to justice."

www.ingramcontent.com/pod-product-compliance
Lightning Source LLC
Chambersburg PA
CBHW070915180626
46817CB00003B/1073